MYSTERIES IN OUR NATIONAL PARKS

MYSTERY
#2

CLIFF-HANGER

GLORIA SKURZYNSKI AND ALANE FERGUSON

NATIONAL GEOGRAPHIC SOCIETY
WASHINGTON, D.C.

To Joni Alm

beloved daughter, sister, and friend.
Everything blooms under your touch.

Maps by Carl Mehler, Director of Maps;
Thomas L. Gray, Map Research; Jehan Aziz and Michelle H. Picard, Map Production
Book design by Ivy Pages.

The cougar used as a design element throughout this book
is from a photograph of a petroglyph taken by George F. Mobley, NGP.
The petroglyph is carved into a sandstone wall near the Four Corners area
of Utah, Colorado, New Mexico, and Arizona.

The legend on pages 93–96 is adapted from "The Children and the Hummingbird"
in *Spider Woman Stories*, by G. M. Mullett. Copyright © 1979 The Arizona Board of Regents.
Reprinted by permission of the
University of Arizona Press and Daisy Mullett Smith.

This is a work of fiction. Any resemblance to
living persons or events other than descriptions of natural
phenomena is purely coincidental.

Library of Congress Cataloging-in-Publication Data
Skurzynski, Gloria
  Cliff-Hanger / by Gloria Skurzynski and Alane Ferguson
    p. cm.—(A national parks mystery ; #2)
  Summary: Twelve-year-old Jack and his younger sister visit Mesa Verde National Park, where they
delve into the park's history while gradually uncovering the mysterious past of their family's teenage foster
child Lucky.
    ISBN 0-7922-7036-3 (hardcover)
    ISBN 0-7922-7654-X (paperback)
    1. Foster home care—Fiction.   2. Mesa Verde National Park—Fiction.
  3. National Parks and Reserves—Fiction.   4. Mystery and detective stories—Fiction.

  I. Ferguson, Alane. II. Title. III. Series.
PZ7.S6287Wcl   1999   98-8716
[Fic]—DC21

Printed in the United States of America

ACKNOWLEDGMENTS

The authors are extremely grateful to the staff

and rangers at Mesa Verde National Park

for all their generous and gracious help:

Larry Wiese, park superintendent;

Will Morris, chief interpretive ranger;

Linda Martin, supervisory park ranger;

Kathy Fiero, archaeologist; Marilyn Colyer, naturalist;

and Jane Anderson, Steve LaPointe,

Nancy Lomayaktewa, Patrick Joshevama,

Tsuyesua Kelhoyouma, Clyde Benally, Chad Benally,

John Lenihan, Mona Hutchinson, and Gretchen Ward.

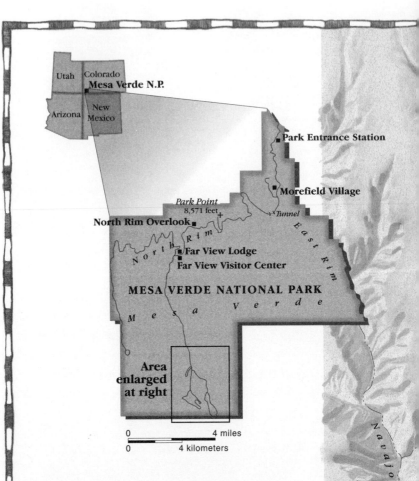

Utah

Colorado
Mesa Verde N.P.

Arizona

New
Mexico

Park Entrance Station

Morefield Village

Park Point
8,571 feet

Tunnel

North Rim Overlook

North Rim

East Rim

Far View Lodge

Far View Visitor Center

MESA VERDE NATIONAL PARK

Mesa Verde

Area
enlarged
at right

0   4 miles
0   4 kilometers

Navajo Canyon

MESA VERDE NATIONAL PARK

PARK DATA

STATE: Colorado   **ESTABLISHED:** 1906

AREA: 52,074 acres

HIGHEST POINT: Park Point, 8,571 feet, with views
of the Four Corners region, where four
states meet

NATURAL FEATURES: Alcoves formed by water
seeping into soft porous sandstone, splitting
away sections of rock. Cliff houses were built
in these alcoves by the ancestral Puebloans.

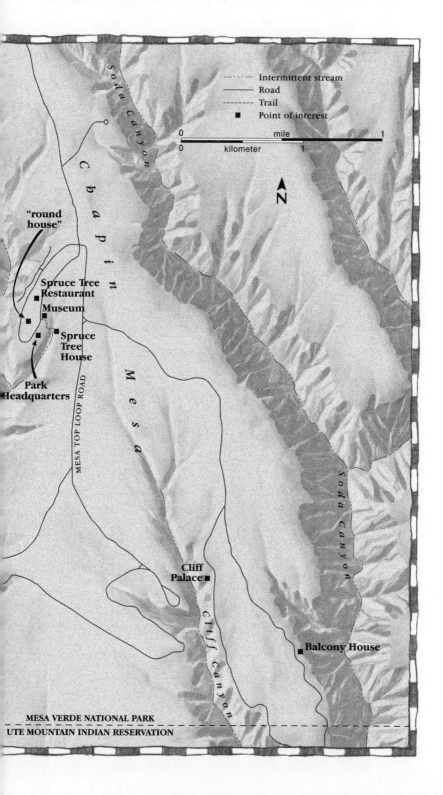

Intermittent stream
Road
Trail
■ Point of interest

0   mile   1
0   kilometer   1

N

Soda Canyon

C h a p i n

"round house"

■ Spruce Tree
Restaurant
Museum ■
■ Spruce Tree
House

Park
Headquarters

M e s a

MESA TOP LOOP ROAD

Soda Canyon

Cliff
Palace ■

Balcony House ■

C l i f f   C a n y o n

MESA VERDE NATIONAL PARK
UTE MOUNTAIN INDIAN RESERVATION

A pair of uniformed officers scanned the truck-stop restaurant, their guns snug in their holsters. Moving only his eyes, the man in the booth looked around. Nearby, a group of ranchers joked with a waitress, who held a full tray perched on her hip.

Pushing his fingertips against his forehead, the man quickly lowered his head. "Behind you. Cops. Two of them," he said softly to the girl with him.

"Are they on to you?" she asked.

"I don't know." Reaching across the table, he gave her hand a quick, hard squeeze. "But I can't take the chance. I'm sorry, baby. You know what you have to do. Make it good."

The man stood. The girl waited until the waitress was only a foot away from their booth. Suddenly the girl shot to her feet, colliding with the loaded tray. Soup, salad, and drinks went flying. Dishes crashed to the *floor, shattering into pieces.*

"Look what you did!" the girl screamed at the waitress. "I'm burned! The soup scalded my skin!" Shrieking, she fell to her knees. All eyes were on her as the man moved toward the door. No one saw him leave.

No one but the girl.

CHAPTER ONE

The sheer cliffs of Mesa Verde cut into the thin, blue air like the blade of an ax. Jack stared at the photograph of the bluff, with its sand-colored stone splintered by fingers of juniper and pine. It was there that the Ancient Ones had once lived. The Ancestral Puebloans. The People. Against all laws of gravity, they had built their homes on ledges that crowned the mesa. Imagining what it must have been like to live on those dizzying cliffs, Jack traced his finger along the picture to the valley 500 feet below. He envisioned himself as one of the People, a warrior who hunted deer and carried his kill across his shoulders, returning to feed his family. Jack looked again at the impossibly narrow path that led to the cliff dwellings. One false step, he realized, and he would have fallen off the side and been crushed onto the valley floor.

"I've got news!" The bedroom door banged as Jack's

sister burst into the room, flushed with excitement. Ashley leaped onto his bed and gave it a hard bounce, which sent Jack's *Photography Today* magazine flying. "You want to hear?"

"Wait a minute. Aren't you supposed to knock?"

"I know. But this is important! It's about our trip to Mesa Verde National Park and the killer cougar."

"Hold on—the cougar didn't kill anybody."

"Whatever. The point is, something's happened that's going to change our whole plan!"

"What?" Jack felt his stomach tighten. He'd been counting down the hours to the trip, scheduled for the next morning. He didn't like surprises.

"Don't look so grouchy, Jack. This is good." Ashley took a breath, which allowed Jack a moment to catch his own breath, even though he'd hardly said a word. "Mom just got a call. From Social Services."

Immediately, Jack's fists tensed in resistance. He didn't want to hear the words he knew were about to come out of Ashley's mouth, as sure as summer followed spring.

"We're getting a little girl! She's on her way now."

"You call that good news?"

"You know it is. Hey, way to be excited," Ashley told him, shaking her head with disapproval. She was the one who was easy with people, always eager to share her life with someone new. But Jack wasn't so open. Especially now. "Anyway, the best part," Ashley went on, "is that she's coming real soon. As in any minute now."

"We can't get a foster kid tonight," Jack cried. "It'll screw up everything! The rangers at Mesa Verde told Mom that with all the visitors streaming into the park, she needs to get there and calm things down before something worse happens. We can't stay home now."

"Jack, that's what's so great!" Ashley's smile was wide enough to crinkle her cheeks. "We're taking her with us! Mom said the girl was dumped at a truck stop down by Cokeville, and no one else can shelter her right now. It's an emergency, Jack. She's coming here—it's already settled."

"Great. Just great. Now I'll get stuck baby-sitting some little girl, and I'll never get to take any good shots," Jack complained, mentally hanging on to that picture of the cliff dwelling in the photography magazine. It wouldn't do much good to moan about it now, since his parents had already said yes to the foster child.

Sure, it was important to help people in need, but sheltering kids during emergencies often turned Jack's life upside down. He liked things to be neat. Orderly. In place. He wanted to feel in control. Now his trip and his whole life were completely messed up. Well, maybe not his whole life, but—

"Quit looking so mad!" Ashley, whose hair hung down her back in a braided rope, chirped, "Mom says the foster girl won't slow anything down at all. So, are you going to come out into the living room and meet her when she comes, or are you just going to sit here looking like a grump?"

"I don't know." Jack threw his magazine onto the bed where his T-shirts and shorts and socks lay in neat piles, ready to go into his duffel bag. Next to them was his camera with four rolls of film, a package of lens-cleaning tissues, and an extra lens cap, just in case he lost one. "I gotta finish packing," he decided. "I can meet her in the morning."

"Up to you!" Tossing her braid in protest, Ashley left the room.

Jack unzipped his duffel bag and started putting things inside it. *Just because I don't want another foster kid right now, does that make me a bad person?* he wondered, feeling a little guilty. His sister, Ashley, who was only ten and a half, loved it when new kids came crashing into their lives. Their father, Steven Landon, welcomed the extra children—he'd once been a foster kid himself. Their mother, Olivia Landon, would have taken foster children full time, instead of just for short-term emergencies, if she hadn't worked at such a demanding job. Olivia, a veterinarian, frequently was called to national parks to help solve problems concerning wildlife, which was exactly the reason they were heading for Mesa Verde National Park in the morning.

Two days earlier, a cougar had attacked a boy hiking a nature trail. All of Mesa Verde was in an uproar, so the park officials had done what many of the other parks around the country did when they had animal trouble— they'd called Olivia Landon for help.

Often when Olivia traveled to the parks as a consultant, Steven and Jack and Ashley went with her. Now there'd be another person tagging along. Jack sighed. Why did foster kids always need help at the worst possible times?

When everything was stowed inside his duffel, Jack sprawled across the foot of his bed and picked up *Photography Today*. Once more he paged to the picture of the cliff dwellings, trying to figure out whether the photographer who took the picture had used a color filter on his lens. There was so much to learn about photography. His dad was still learning after 20 years behind a camera lens. Jack lost himself in the pages of the magazine, reading article after article about zoom lenses and filters and fancy, expensive tripods.

Once again his door banged open. "I know you're not happy about this, but trust me, Jack. You gotta come," Ashley said. Even though she was trying to speak softly so she wouldn't be overheard, excitement bubbled up through her voice.

"No, I don't gotta," Jack answered.

"But she's here," Ashley murmured. "She's fantastic! Wait till you see her, Jack. Her name's Lucky."

"Sounds like a dog."

"A dog!" Ashley started to giggle. "Some dog. Come

on, Jack. I left her all alone in the living room. Mom and Dad and the social worker are in the kitchen talking—about Lucky, I bet."

"I'm ready for bed."

"Come on—quit stalling." Ashley stomped her foot impatiently. "If you won't come, you're being rude. Lucky really wants to meet you. Rude! Hear me?" The door slammed loudly behind Ashley's retreating figure.

"Yeah, and close the door on your way out," Jack muttered sarcastically. He slid off the bed onto his knees. If Ashley told their parents that he was being impolite to one of the foster kids, he'd get into trouble. "Fine, just...fine! I'll go meet her. Then will everyone just leave me alone?" Grumbling to himself, he pulled on a pair of jeans, but danged if he'd wear shoes. Bare feet ought to be good enough for meeting some little girl named after a dog.

The extra-long T-shirt he used for sleeping hung down almost to his knees, and the jeans were too short because he'd been growing a lot lately, and he'd already packed his new ones. As he glanced into the mirror, he saw that he looked kind of weird, but he didn't care. Barefoot and tousle haired, with a droopy shirt and outgrown jeans, he slouched down the hall to the living room.

At first he didn't see her. Then he heard her voice. "You're Jack, right?" she asked, smiling.

Perfect white teeth. Warm smile. Jack barely registered the dimples because his attention was caught by her eyes—fringed with thick, dark lashes and as green as the four-leaf clover she wore on a chain around her neck. He'd never, not once in his whole life, seen anything—*anyone*—like her.

"It's great to meet you," Lucky told him softly.

Stunned, he blurted, "They said you were a little kid! How old are you?" and immediately felt like a jerk. What a way to start a conversation!

"Sorry to disappoint you. I'm thirteen," she answered. "And you're what? Fifteen?"

Ashley burst out laughing. "Fifteen! Come on, Lucky. He's only twelve."

Jack stammered, "I'm practically thirteen."

"Practically? Oh, yeah, right," Ashley snorted. "You won't be thirteen till—"

Before Ashley could finish, Lucky broke in, "I bet I thought you were older because you're so tall. You're a whole lot taller than I am. You could pass for high school, easy."

He straightened his spine as far as it would go until he realized that stretching himself made his too-short jeans rise up even higher above his ankles.

"I bet you're glad you came to meet her now, aren't you?" Ashley snickered, "Some dog, huh, Jack?"

Still smiling, but looking puzzled, Lucky asked, "Dog? What do you mean?"

"Oh, just that my dumb brother Jack said that with a name like Lucky, you must be a—"

Jack leaped to his feet so fast he felt his own teeth

rattle. He grabbed his sister's arm and growled, "Come with me, Ashley. Now!"

"Why? Where?"

"We're going to get Lucky a drink."

"That would be great," Lucky murmured. "A Coke, if you've got one. Or, water's fine."

Ashley writhed under Jack's grip as she argued, "Both of us don't need to go...."

"Yes, we do!" Eyes blazing, Jack dragged his sister into the hall.

"What's wrong with you?" she demanded. "What did I do?"

He lit into her with a hissing tirade of furiously whispered words, telling her how she'd humiliated him and that she'd just better figure out when to keep her mouth shut if she knew what was good for her. Stung, Ashley looked at him, wide-eyed. "I was only teasing, Jack. Geesh, when did you get so sensitive?"

Clamping her arm even tighter, Jack ordered, "I don't want you embarrassing me in front of Lucky. Now, you go back into that living room and talk nice to her while I get the drink. But don't you say one word about me to her. Don't even think about it. Got it?"

"Who wants to?" For the third time in an hour, Ashley flounced off. Glowering, he watched her go. Then he turned toward the kitchen. Almost at the door, he stopped abruptly because he heard the social worker mentioning Lucky's name.

"...such a beautiful girl," Ms. Lopez was saying. "That hair—all those auburn curls!"

"Yes, she's very pretty," Olivia agreed.

Ms. Lopez continued, "And as striking as Lucky is, you'd think someone somewhere would have noticed her and remembered her. But the police can't track her, and she won't tell us anything about herself except for that ridiculous name. Lucky Deal—what kind of a name is that?"

"Obviously fake," Steven answered.

"Making it impossible to trace," Ms. Lopez added.

Jack knew it was wrong to eavesdrop, but he couldn't stop himself. He stayed hidden behind the wall, listening intently as Ms. Lopez talked to his parents.

"She's a charmer, but at times she can act quite odd. We'd interrogated her—unsuccessfully, I might add—and we'd begun filling out the papers to bring her here. All of a sudden she jumped up and demanded to make a phone call. It had to be right then, she insisted, that very minute. She created a huge fuss, yelling that even if she was a juvenile, she was entitled to one phone call."

"Was she?" Olivia asked.

"No, but we let her use the phone anyway. Since she refused to tell us who she was calling, we wanted to trace it."

"Who was it to?" Steven wondered.

"We didn't find out. But we do know she dialed the number of a phone booth in Park City, Utah."

Hesitating, Jack decided this was not the time to walk into the kitchen and rummage through the refrigerator for a soft drink. The last words he heard as he turned away were a warning from Ms. Lopez.

"It sounds as if your assignment at Mesa Verde is an important one, Olivia, and I can't tell you how grateful we are that you're willing to include Lucky in your plans at the last minute like this. Our agency is hoping that a trip to a beautiful park might be just the distraction she needs to let down her defenses and tell you about herself. But...."

"But what?" Olivia asked.

"You'll need to be careful. There's something not quite right about Lucky."

"Meaning?" Steven asked.

"Meaning—watch your back. Lucky's a handful. Cougars aren't the only creatures that can turn on you."

CHAPTER TWO

Jack tossed restlessly. Lying flat on the edge of the cliff, he clutched brittle rock with his fingernails as he stared down a vast chasm to the canyon floor. Then the rock crumbled into sand, shattering his safe handhold, plunging him into peril. He was falling. He heard the wind, heard Lucky's voice whisper, "Mesa Verde." Or maybe it was the wind that sighed the words as they streamed around him: "Flying. Flying. To Colorado."

With a start, he rose out of the terrifying plunge of his dream to find his fingers curled stiffly around the edge of his quilt. Still, the soft voice whispered inside his head, even after he convinced himself he was awake and was no longer dreaming. Jack rolled out of his bed onto his feet and padded to the bedroom door, opening it just a crack.

A small, arched alcove in the hall held one of the Landons' telephones. Lucky stood there, hunched over, cradling the receiver, speaking in low tones with her back turned toward Jack's door. Barefoot, she'd wrapped herself in a terry cloth robe Olivia had lent her. As she pressed the phone against her ear, the robe's full sleeve slid back to reveal her wristwatch. Jack had noticed the watch earlier in the evening. He remembered thinking then that it was a large, chunky-looking one for a girl to wear. More like a man's. Now he could easily read the glowing digital numbers: 2:10 a.m. The middle of the night.

"It'll be OK," she was saying softly. "Don't worry so much. I can handle them."

She hung up then. When she turned around and noticed Jack, she jumped in surprise. No smile this time: Her startled eyes turned as cold as green ice. "What did you hear?" she demanded.

He stammered, "Nothing. Just, like, something about you can handle—I don't know what." His eyebrows drew together as his mind focused on her and on the telephone that now lay back in its cradle. She shouldn't be here, calling someone in secret. The last of his sleepiness evaporated as his mind finally comprehended what was happening. "Wait, what are you doing? Who were you calling?"

It seemed to Jack that a lot of different looks flitted across Lucky's face, as if she were searching for the right one. Suddenly, her face turned soft, pleading.

"Shhhh!" She pointed toward Steven and Olivia's

bedroom door. "Quiet! Please?" Then, gesturing toward the living room, she tiptoed down the hall, away from where the rest of the Landons were sleeping. Jack followed, not sure what he should do, but knowing he could call out for his folks in an instant if he needed them. For now, he wanted to understand what Lucky was up to.

She motioned for him to sit on the couch, then perched on a footstool opposite him, gazing at him like someone about to ask a favor. Keep it together, Jack warned himself. Stay cool. Get information. "So," he asked softly. "What's going on?"

"I...I don't know if I can tell you," she whispered. Then, a beat later, she added, "I don't know if I should."

"What is it?"

Lucky stayed silent.

"Is it something bad?"

"Yes."

Bad! Jack's stomach squeezed. With a foster kid that could mean all kinds of things, problems that Jack wouldn't know how to deal with. "Listen," he began, "maybe I should get my folks—"

"No!" Lucky said the word with such force that Jack blinked. "I'm sorry, it's just—I need to tell someone, and I thought, since you're so...." She took a breath, then shook her head. "But not anyone else—not your folks and not the social workers. Your mom's already all upset about the cougar and all the problems at Mesa Verde.

She couldn't handle this, too. She'd send me back, and that could get me killed."

"Killed! Wait a minute, wait a minute. I don't get this. I need to go one step at a time. Who was on the phone?"

"Maria. She's my friend from where I used to live."

Jack turned on a small table lamp, which sent a flare of light through the room. He had to be able to see her better, to make sense of the words going into his head. "Maria—is she the one who's trying to hurt you?"

"No. Jack, Maria was almost killed by gang members."

"Gang members?"

"We were together—Maria and me—when we saw the gang do a crime. They found us out." Lucky squeezed her eyes shut, but continued. "We tried to run, but they caught us and said that if we ever told, they'd find us both and kill us. Maria started screaming. They didn't like that. They beat her up real, real bad." She shuddered, barely whispering the last words. "I was faster. I got away."

"Gang members?" Jack knew he sounded incredulous, but he couldn't help it. Ms. Lopez had warned his parents to be careful of Lucky. Maybe he should be, too. His thoughts must have shown on his face, because suddenly, her green eyes pierced him like a laser. "You think I'm lying? You think I'm making this whole thing up?"

Now it was Jack's turn to stay silent.

"You want me to prove it? Is that what it takes for you to believe?" Pulling up the right sleeve of the robe,

Lucky revealed a nasty bruise, like an ugly shadow, on her forearm. "They gave me this," she told him.

She must have been hit, and hit hard. Nothing short of a hard punch could have left such a mark. Quickly, Lucky pulled the sleeve back down and looked up at him again with her eyes wide. Stunned, Jack stared back. "I'm sorry," was all he could think to say.

"When I first met you, Jack, I thought I could trust you. But I guess you're not any different from everyone else. You need proof. If a bruise is what it takes for you to know I'm telling the truth, then I guess that's what it takes. I want you to believe me. I need you to."

"I do." Living in Jackson Hole, Jack didn't see much of the harsher side of life that some of their foster kids had dealt with every day. Jack's own life was safe and well ordered. His mother and father cocooned him in love in a way that seemed quite ordinary to Jack, until he peered into others' lives and saw the turmoil and pain. He should never forget just how fortunate he was.

"You know what bothers me the most?" Lucky asked him.

"What?"

"It bothers me when I think that it should have been me that's in the hospital. Not Maria. I got away because I'm quick."

"Lucky, you can't feel bad about that. Things just...happen. I'm glad you made it."

"But it's not fair," she wailed softly. "That's why I

have to call her, so I know she's OK. I feel so guilty!"
Hugging her sides tightly, Lucky crumpled into herself.
"You know what just happened? Maria told me that the
gang left a message. She said they're still looking for
me, and if I come back, I'm dead. That's when I told
her not to worry, that I could handle them. But the truth
is, I'm scared."

Perplexed, Jack asked, "What about the police? Tell
them what's going on. They'd protect you."

Lucky shook her head and gave Jack a look full of
pity. "You don't know much about gangs, Jack. They
have spies everywhere. You might not believe this, but
some cops are gang members. I don't trust anyone anymore." She drew in a breath, then placed her hand
lightly on his. "Except, maybe, you. I think I can trust
you. You won't tell anyone about Maria, will you Jack?"

"But my parents—"

"If you tell them, they've got to go to Social
Services. It's their responsibility. If you don't say
anything, then they won't have to make that decision.
It'd be like you're protecting your parents, too."

Jack figured that if his mother and father found out
Lucky had made a call, they'd be bound by law to tell
Ms. Lopez. It was better, Jack decided, to protect all of
them. "I won't tell," he promised.

"Not Ashley, either? She seems sweet, but I don't
want her to worry—"

"Especially Ashley," Jack added hastily. "You don't

know her yet, but she's a blabbermouth. No, I won't tell a soul."

"Good. Thanks, Jack," she breathed. "You just saved my life."

What was he supposed to say to that? "Uh...I didn't really...I mean....Hey, is all your stuff packed? We're leaving for Mesa Verde pretty early, like in five hours. We ought to get some sleep."

"All right. Good night, Jack," she answered. "And...thanks! So much."

Jack hurried down the hall to his room. Now it was 2:35 a.m. The red digital numbers on his bedroom clock pulsed second after second; he squeezed his eyelids tight, wondering how he'd ever get back to sleep.

He couldn't erase the image of Lucky gazing up at him with those big green eyes, looking so defenseless—on the outside. But what was she like on the inside? He remembered Ms. Lopez telling his parents they should watch her. He pictured prim, kindly, gray-haired Ms. Lopez—not the kind of woman to make things up, but, then again, not a woman who'd known the whole story. Lucky could have confided in Ms. Lopez, but she hadn't. She'd trusted Jack. Only him.

Flipping onto his stomach, he burrowed his face deep in the pillow. Whatever happened, he knew he was on Lucky's side.

CHAPTER THREE

They flew in a deHavilland jet from their hometown of Jackson Hole, Wyoming, to Denver, Colorado. That particular plane had eight rows of two seats each on both sides of the aisle. "Would you rather have an aisle or a window seat?" Lucky asked Jack. Did that mean she wanted to sit next to him? he wondered.

"Go ahead, sit right there, Jack," his mother told him. "Dad and I will be across the aisle from you two, and Ashley can have the seat in front of you. There are plenty of empty seats."

Feeling awkward, noticing how bony his knees looked—why had he worn shorts?—Jack slid into the seat next to Lucky. "Good. We can talk," she said, feeling for the seat belt. Jack moved away from her, mashing himself against the armrest.

She stayed silent while the plane took off from Jackson airport, while the flight attendant went over all the instructions about what to do in case of an emergency, and even after the Fasten Seat Belt sign went off. Jack searched his brain for something to say, something that wouldn't sound stupid. He thought of giving Lucky more details about the cougar attack at Mesa Verde, but he remembered Lucky's bruise and decided he didn't want to talk about any kind of assault. Maybe he could ask her about Maria. No, Jack doubted he could talk without being overheard, which meant he'd better save that topic for another time. He was just about to ask Lucky if she'd been following the NBA basketball play-offs when Ashley's face popped up over the back of the seat in front of them.

Ashley crossed her arms on the top of the seat, planted her chin on her arms, looked brightly at Lucky, and asked straight out, "How'd you ever get a nick-name like that? Is it your real name? I never heard of anyone named Lucky."

Jack gave Ashley his fiercest, big brother "keep quiet" stare, but Lucky only laughed and answered, "I never heard of anyone else either. I'll tell you how it happened: I was about five years old. We were living in Las Vegas, and I wanted to play one of the slot machines because they looked really fun. You know— all those cherries and plums and lemons whirling around. You know, Jack?"

He really didn't. He'd never seen an actual slot machine—only a video game his friend had.

Lucky went on, "My dad said, 'Lacey, the slots are a sucker's game. Don't waste that shiny quarter I gave you on the slots. Buy a pack of gum. At least you'll have something for your money.'"

Jack and Ashley exchanged glances. So her real name was Lacey! Their parents didn't know that, and even the social worker, Ms. Lopez, hadn't been able to find out Lucky's name. And now she'd slipped up and said it right out loud.

"But I kept begging my dad—please, please, please!—and finally he let me play a quarter. 'Just one quarter,' he said. 'That's all.'"

"So what happened?" Ashley asked, wide-eyed.

"I hit a hundred-dollar jackpot. All these quarters came tumbling out of the machine and fell all over the floor."

"Wow!" Ashley exclaimed, impressed, but Jack asked, "Isn't it illegal for kids under eighteen to gamble in Las Vegas?"

"Sure," Lucky answered, grinning at him. "But the guards didn't catch me—my dad made sure of that. So then, while we were picking up the quarters, my dad told me, 'From now on I'm going to call you Lucky. You're my good-luck charm.' Right after that he bought me this." She touched the four-leaf clover pendant that hung around her neck.

From across the aisle Olivia said, "Ashley, sit down the right way. You need to face forward."

"I will in a minute, Mom. Just give me one more minute." Grimacing, Ashley said, "Moms! They're always bugging you. Hey, Lucky, what did your mom think? I mean, did she get mad 'cause your dad let you do something illegal?"

For a long moment Lucky looked out the window. When she turned back toward them, her large green eyes brimmed with tears. "My mother was already dead by then."

"Oh!" Ashley murmured, dropping lower in her seat. "How...how did she die?"

Lucky answered in a husky voice, "She worked as a magician's assistant in a big Las Vegas show. She was so good! But one night while they were performing, the magician's white tiger mauled her. She died from the wounds." The tears welled up even more, spilling over Lucky's lower lids, running in rivulets down her cheeks.

"That's so awful!" Ashley wailed.

Steven Landon reached across the aisle and tapped his daughter's shoulder. "You need to sit down, Ashley. If we hit any unexpected turbulence, you could bounce right up and slam against the ceiling. People get hurt bad that way."

As Ashley sank into her seat, Lucky rubbed the tears from her cheeks. "Do you have a tissue?" she asked Jack.

Fumbling in the pockets of his shorts, he searched for something that could wipe up tears. A rumpled Kleenex—it didn't have to look brand new, as long as it was clean. But all he could find was a cash-register receipt for a Slurpee from 7-Eleven. "Sorry," he mumbled, with honest regret.

"It doesn't matter. I just get...emotional...when I think about my mother," she murmured.

"Yeah. Sure. No wonder."

Lucky leaned forward, "Excuse me, Jack. I'll just slip out to the lavatory and get myself a tissue."

"OK." Jack swung around and hung his knees over the armrest so that his feet, in their big sneakers, dangled in the aisle. The corners of Lucky's lips twitched ever so slightly with amusement as she moved past him. When she was gone, Jack smacked his forehead with the heels of his hands. Why hadn't he stood up to let her get past! That's what he should have done—stand up, step into the aisle, and get out of her way. He groaned inwardly. How stupid his feet had looked dangling in midair! Why did he keep coming off so geeky?

"Mom, Dad!" Now Ashley was in the aisle.

"Can't you just sit still?" her father demanded. "You keep bobbing up and down. Your mother's trying to work out a plan for Mesa Verde. It's important, Ashley. Some people have even demanded that the cougars be taken out of the park."

"Taken out?" Ashley cried. "They can't do that, can they?"

Olivia looked up from a stack of papers she'd been reading and patted Ashley's hand. "No, but it shows you how scared folks get when they realize the damage a wild animal can do. Anyway, what did you need to tell us?"

"Oh, yeah. Well, it's about Lucky." Leaning over her parents and talking in a loud stage whisper, Ashley told them, "I know how you can find out who she is. First, her real name's Lacey. Second, her mother got attacked by a magician's white tiger in Las Vegas."

"Oh, Ashley!" Olivia looked pityingly at her daughter.

"A white tiger?" Steven exclaimed, and laughed out loud. "She's feeding you a story, sweetheart."

"Honest, Dad! You should have seen her. She was crying and everything when she told us about it. Wasn't she, Jack?"

Hesitant, Jack nodded.

"I mean," Ashley went on, "how many people get killed by a white tiger in a big Las Vegas show? It must have been in all the papers, don't you think? You could check it out real easy, even though it happened—let's see—at least eight years ago."

Olivia turned to Jack and asked, "What do you think, Jack? Do you buy into that fantastic story?"

What did he think? He believed it. No one could fake tears like that. Lucky had to be telling the truth. But if Jack admitted that and they were able to trace Lucky's background, she'd be returned to wherever it was the gang was waiting to hurt her.

"I...I don't know."

Olivia sighed. "OK. When we change planes at the Denver airport, I'll call Ms. Lopez and tell her what you just said. We'll see what she can find out. Now, kids, let me get back to my reading. I'm almost out of time, and I've got to learn everything I can about what happened at Mesa Verde."

In one of the molded plastic seats in the Denver airport terminal, Jack found the sports section of that day's *Denver Post*. Since someone had left it behind, he supposed it was OK for him to pick it up and read it. That evening the Utah Jazz— Jack's favorite team— would be in the NBA play-offs. Jack read the predictions about who would win, including the Las Vegas odds: four to three, favoring the Jazz in the series.

If gambling odds could be printed in the paper, Jack thought, trying to convince himself, it probably wasn't so bad that Lucky had played the slot machine. Just that once, when she was little and probably didn't know any better. Especially since she didn't have a mother to keep an eye on her.

He checked his watch. They'd be boarding in about twenty minutes, getting onto the smaller plane that would fly them from Denver to Durango. He looked around for his family. His father was watching the news on the television monitor mounted just beneath the ceiling. His mother was walking toward a bank of pay phones.

Curious, because maybe she was going to call Ms.

Lopez about Lucky, Jack made his way toward the phones, sidestepping through throngs of travelers in the busy airport. For a few minutes they kept him from seeing his mother. When he caught sight of her, she was punching numbers into the telephone keypad. Lucky stood close behind her.

Oddly close. Slightly to the side. She seemed to be staring intently at Olivia's fingers as they dialed.

"What's she doing?" Ashley asked from right beside Jack.

"Where'd you come from? And what do you mean? What's who doing?"

"You know who I mean—Lucky. She's practically on top of Mom, but Mom doesn't know she's back there. I bet Lucky's trying to hear what Mom's saying on the phone."

"Mom hasn't started talking yet," Jack protested.

"Well, when she starts. I better get over there. If Lucky hears Mom talking to Ms. Lopez, she'll know I squealed on her."

Ashley darted through the crowd until she reached Lucky. The two of them immediately walked off together, so if Lucky had been trying to eavesdrop, she hadn't heard much.

The plane they flew in to Durango had only 21 seats, total, in rows of two seats together on one side and single seats on the other. Ashley sat with Steven, Lucky with Olivia, and Jack was by himself in one of the single seats across from Lucky, with no one to talk to and a lot of time to think.

He took out his camera from his backpack and loaded a roll of film. As soon as they got settled at Mesa Verde National Park, he was going to ask Lucky if he could take her picture. Until now, Jack hadn't been at all interested in taking pictures of people. Like his dad, he liked to shoot wildlife— with a camera. A couple of times he'd tried to take pictures of football games or hockey, but he never seemed to click the shutter at just the right fraction of a second. His sports pictures always turned out wrong, with one player's arm across another player's face, or a blurry streak where someone had raced past his lens.

Now he wanted to photograph Lucky. Watching her out of the corner of his eye so she wouldn't catch him staring, he thought about how he'd frame her against the cliff dwellings at Mesa Verde. He wished he'd brought his photography magazine; it had an article about shooting portraits in a landscape environment.

"Here we are," Olivia announced as they climbed down the stairs from the plane onto the tarmac— Durango was too small an airport to have a Jetway. "Durango, Colorado."

"You get the baggage, Jack," Steven told him.

When they entered the building, Lucky turned around as if she were looking for something. "I have to find a rest room," she announced.

Pointing to a sign, Olivia said, "Over that way. Don't be too long, though. We'll meet you at the rental car desk, and then we're off to Mesa Verde."

"You bet. I can't wait!" With a small wave, Lucky moved quickly down the corridor.

"Hold on, Lucky," Ashley called out. "I'll go with you."

Lucky turned, and Jack saw another whisper of a look—maybe impatience or maybe even anger—pass across her face. "I'd like to go alone, if you don't mind," she said sharply.

"Why?" Ashley asked.

It seemed as though Lucky couldn't come up with an answer. She stared at Ashley, stone-faced, her mouth pressed into a straight line. Olivia, sensing Lucky's annoyance, cheerily said, "How about this—I'll go with the two of you."

A beat of silence, followed by a terse "Fine" from Lucky.

As the three of them disappeared down the hall-way, Jack turned the scene over in his mind. The whole interaction between Ashley and Lucky and his mother had been odd. Why was Lucky resisting their company? Suddenly, the answer hit him: She must have wanted to break free and find a pay phone so she could check on Maria. That had to be it. He smiled to himself, warmed by the secret knowledge that only he and Lucky shared. In a way, it was hard being the one person who understood her whole story. The rest of the Landons were bound to find her behavior strange, which concerned him. Still, he'd vowed to keep her secret, and he meant to honor that promise.

For some reason it always seemed to take a lot longer for luggage to be unloaded at a small airport than at a large one. Jack stood watching the empty conveyor belt snake its lazy way around its track until the first bags appeared. A large cooler with duct tape wrapped in silver stripes pushed through the baggage opening, followed by two flowered totes and a green suitcase with wheels. Jack had just spied one of the Landon bags when a "Hey!" behind him made him jump.

Whirling around, Jack almost bumped into his sister. "Ashley, where's Lucky?"

"Still with Mom. I want to tell you something weird. About Lucky."

"What about her?"

"I don't know how to say it. It was just...kind of strange, the way she was acting. For one thing, she kept looking around her all the way to the rest room. Up front, sideways, but she was only moving her eyes, like she didn't want anyone to know she was checking the place out."

Jack felt a surge of impatience. "So? Is that supposed to mean something?"

"Well, I'm wondering if she used to live here."

"That's not it." Jack jerked his mother's suitcase off the conveyor belt and set it down hard.

"You don't know that," Ashley said, her voice rising. "And why are you getting so touchy? I thought maybe you'd seen the same thing, and we could tell Mom and Dad and then maybe they could find out if Durango is her real home."

"What is it with you, Ashley?" he demanded, grabbing another bag. "It's like you've turned into a spy or something. Why don't you just leave her alone?"

Now it was Ashley's turn to look at him in stony silence. She might have said more, but right then Steven walked up. "Great. Our luggage made it. You two wait here with the suitcases while I go pick up the rental car."

"What kind of car did you get, Dad? Is it a red one?" Ashley asked hopefully.

"Yeah. A Lamborghini," Jack added.

"No, we can't fit in that, so pick a Rolls Royce," Ashley joked.

"A Hummer." Jack was getting into the spirit of it, glad the tension with his sister was melting. "A Hummer with Utah Jazz seat covers and its own television and VCR inside."

Steven laughed. "You got it. I'll make it a red one. Meet me out front, guys."

CHAPTER FOUR

It turned out to be a white Ford Taurus, just like most of the other rental cars—not that Jack had expected anything racier.

Ashley wedged herself into the middle of the back-seat between Jack and Lucky. Jack had to peer around his sister every time he wanted to say something to Lucky. That didn't happen often, because Olivia kept up a steady stream of talk.

"Isn't this a beautiful place? It's a lot more mountain-ous than Jackson Hole, although I think they're close to the same altitude. Which reminds me, Jack and Ashley, both of you have to write reports since you're miss-ing school. Ashley, yours is to be on an animal that lives in Mesa Verde, right?"

"Uh-huh."

Olivia turned around from the front seat. "There are a lot of interesting animals in this park—coyotes and badgers and lots of mule deer and elk. Have you ever stood next to an elk, Lucky?"

When Lucky shook her head no, Olivia slipped right into her lecture mode. She loved to share information about her job at the National Elk Refuge. "Well, let me tell you, they are huge! A lot bigger than you might think. My head stops right at a bull elk's shoulder, if you can picture that."

"Mom, I don't want to do a report on elk," Ashley broke in. "What else is there? Give me something with teeth."

"OK, how about a black bear? They have them in Mesa Verde. And, of course, the cougar. Did you know the cougar is also called a mountain lion and a puma? They've got several names for the exact same animal. That might be interesting to mention, Ashley, if you do your paper on *Felis concolor*, which is, as you can probably guess, the scientific name for a cougar." Olivia was growing excited. "Hey, really, cougars would be great for you to write on, since I've already gathered a lot of information. I could highlight some of the data...."

Ashley rolled her eyes at Jack to show she did not want to talk about school reports. Jack agreed. What was the use of getting a couple of days off if they had to worry about homework right from the start? Homework could wait. School would be over at the beginning of June—just two more weeks.

"How do you know about all those animals, Mrs. Landon?" Lucky asked.

"It's my job. I specialize in endangered and threatened species. You heard about the cougar attack I've been called to investigate?"

Lucky nodded. "I heard a little, but not much. What's going on?"

Running her fingers through her hair, Olivia sighed. "It's really tragic, Lucky. Last week a little boy was walking with his family down a trail, and he got too far ahead of them. There was a scream. When the parents came around the bend...." She paused, shaking her head. "It's not the way cougars usually behave. That's what's so frightening."

"Was the boy all right?" Lucky asked.

"He had quite a few bites around his face, but I understand he'll make it. The park hunted down the cougar and caught it. I was asked to examine it, to check for disease or age or any other cause that could explain such an attack."

Olivia turned back toward the front of the car but twisted around again when Lucky said, "I bet it took lots of years in school to learn all that you know about animals."

"Uh-huh. A whole bunch of years," Olivia admitted. "But it doesn't seem long when you're doing something you love." She paused, then asked, "Where do you go to school?"

Lucky didn't miss a beat. "Home schooling."

"Where's your home?"

Lucky shrugged and smiled. "Wherever."

"Do you travel a lot?" Olivia pressed.

"Mom!" Jack protested. Talk about a grilling! His mom was sounding like the FBI. Next she'd be pulling out the truth serum. "Lucky doesn't have to answer that," Jack said.

"Actually, I'd rather not," Lucky murmured, very polite and still smiling.

Olivia took the hint and turned again toward the front to talk to Steven. Ashley, who was usually a chatterbox, was silent for a change. Jack could see she was chewing over these newest crumbs of noninformation Lucky had just spilled, although there wasn't much to digest.

No one spoke for a while. Jack watched the minutes tick by on his watch and the high mountains fly past the car windows. Those peaks looked as sharp and white as a wolf's teeth. After a while they gave way to a wide valley, and then, farther south, a different kind of elevation. Lucky exclaimed, "That mountain over there looks like a sphinx."

"It's called a mesa, not a mountain," Ashley said a bit testily. "'Mesa Verde' is Spanish for 'green table.' A mesa isn't the same as a mountain."

"Well, it sort of is." Jack knew why his sister was sounding peevish. Ashley tended to get carsick, and the curling route was guaranteed to make even someone with an iron stomach feel queasy. "Here, trade places with me," he suggested. "You'll feel better next to the window."

The narrow road that led to Mesa Verde wound higher and higher, as though a long ribbon had been carelessly tossed onto the mesa's spine. Back and forth the Landons went, twisting around one hairpin turn after another.

"You don't look too good," Lucky told Ashley. "Are you OK?"

"I'll be all right as soon as we stop moving," she answered through gritted teeth. Ashley, who felt nauseated during ordinary drives, clung to the door in agony. The window was rolled down a third of the way so she could drink in fresh air, but Jack could tell by her gray pallor that it wasn't helping. Since Ashley was smashed against the car door, there was plenty of room in the backseat for Lucky and Jack to spread out.

"Tunnel coming up," Steven announced. Before the words were out of his dad's mouth, Jack found himself in utter blackness. He blinked hard. His eyes couldn't adjust to more than the tiny strips of lights on the tunnel floor and the small, baseball-size circle of light at the other end.

"Ohhh, I can't see a thing!" Lucky cried. "I hate it when it's so dark—spooks me out!"

And then he felt it. She was holding his hand! Before he even had time to think about what was happening, the tunnel ended and the car burst into the light again. Lucky pulled away. But when she looked at him with a shy smile, Jack understood what she was saying: There was another link between the two of them.

Another secret Jack and Lucky shared.

"Hey, what happened to the trees?" Lucky asked, peering out the window. "They're all burned."

"A huge fire was started by a lightning strike in 1996," Olivia explained. "The damage looks devastating—and it was—but there's an exciting part to it. The burn areas revealed a lot of archaeological sites that haven't been excavated yet. They're like a treasure trove, just waiting to be discovered."

Lucky leaned closer to the front seat. "You said treasure. You mean there are jewels and stuff lying around that they haven't dug up?"

This time Steven answered. "No, not that kind of treasure. Things like pots and tools and jewelry. They're valuable because they reveal the history of the people who were here 800 years ago."

Lucky pursed her lips. "So the stuff out there's not worth any money?"

"I wouldn't say that," Olivia told her. "Years ago, greedy people robbed the sites, sold the artifacts, and made themselves a fortune. But doing that is wrong. The past belongs to the people who used to live here, not to thieves who want to cash in."

Ashley groaned, "Dad, I think I need to stop for a minute. I really feel sick."

Glancing at his daughter in the rearview mirror, Steven said, "OK, honey. Hold on. I'll pull over just as soon as we can. Are you going to make it?"

Clamping her hand over her mouth, Ashley whispered, "Hurry."

When the shoulder of the road widened into a lookout point, Steven stopped the car. He'd barely jerked on the hand brake before Ashley bolted from the backseat. The others followed her.

Charred, twisted tree skeletons marched right up to the road's edge. Fire had leaped across the asphalt to ravage both sides, leaving an ocean of blackened juniper and pinyon pine. It was hard to think the destruction had done any good at all—it looked like nothing more than a graveyard of trees. A path bordered by a wooden fence led up to a lookout point. "Come on, Jack," Lucky told him, playfully pulling on his shirt. "Let's go see what's up there. It looks like Ashley's going to take a while."

He saw his sister bent over, breathing deeply, with their parents at her side. Ashley hadn't thrown up, but she looked as though she could at any minute. "You two stay together," Steven warned. "I don't want you going far from the road."

"No problem, Dad. We'll stay close."

Passing a sign that said North Rim Overlook, Jack and Lucky wandered down the asphalt path to a railing that blocked them from going farther.

"Oh my! Look at that," Lucky gasped. She gripped the rail tightly, even though there was still a wide jut of ledge beneath her. "It's like I can see the whole world."

"Wow," Jack said softly. "It's awesome."

A panorama spread out beneath them, so far away it was as if a giant quilt had been unfurled. Tiny specks that must be houses dotted patches of green, stitched in borders of golden yellow. Patterns of color repeated themselves in the valley as far as their eyes could see.

"Jack, Lucky, we're going now!"

"OK," Jack called back. He knew he should invite his parents to look at the incredible view, but suddenly he didn't want to share it. This was for him and Lucky. "You ready?" he asked her.

They walked toward the car in silence. Along the edges of the road, beneath the dead bones of the trees, grew a fresh blanket of green grasses, punctuated by blue and yellow wildflowers. The forest was healing. Suddenly, Jack felt Lucky pull away.

"Hold on a second," she said. Without more warning than that, she darted into the trees, heading straight for a cluster of blue blossoms.

"No, don't! You're not allowed to go off the path!" Jack cried. "That's a burn area—it's off limits!"

"I just want to pick one flower." She laughed, still running lightly. "What can one hurt?"

"Lucky, for heaven's sake, get back here," Steven ordered. He sounded much more serious than Jack did. Lucky froze, her hand hovering over a patch of blue. Then she crouched low and turned her back toward them, obscuring Jack's view.

Steven called, "You're on a burn area. No one's allowed to walk on it. I told you to stay with Jack."

"I'll only be a minute!"

When Olivia and Ashley joined them, Ashley asked Jack, "What's Lucky doing?"

"Uh, she wanted to pick a wildflower."

"Hey! She can't do that!" Ashley protested.

Grimly, Jack replied, "I know. But she doesn't know about the rules of the parks. I bet she's never been to one before." Even to him the excuse sounded lame. Both he and his dad had told her to come back, yet she hadn't moved. Hunched into a question mark, she seemed to be lost in admiration of the wildflowers.

"Come on, Lucky," Olivia shouted. "You've got to get out of there."

"Just one more second," Lucky called over her shoulder.

"You're going to let her get away with that?" Rolling her eyes, Ashley announced, "Fine. I'll go get her. My feet are small so they won't squish the ground as bad. Hey, Lucky!" she cried. "I'm coming after you."

Gingerly, Ashley picked her way toward the crouching figure. When there were less than five yards between them, Lucky twisted around. As quick as a jackknife snapping open, she jumped to her feet, jamming her fists into her jeans pockets. Head down, she hurried past Ashley, muttering, "Never mind. I'm ready to go." Then, brushing past Olivia, Jack, and Steven, murmuring "sorry" every few seconds, Lucky climbed into the car and slammed the door shut.

For a moment, the Landons stared in silence at the rental car and its occupant. "Well," Steven finally said, scratching the top of his head, "I guess the next time we have any trouble with her we'll know who to send in. At least Ashley gets results. Good job, sweetie," he told his daughter.

Olivia frowned. "Odd," she murmured. Then, shrugging her shoulders, she sighed, "I guess we should just go with whatever works."

"Yep," Steven agreed. "So let's get out of here."

Ashley didn't say anything as she trailed along behind them. In silence she took her post next to the car door, her face clouded, probably in anticipation of the upcoming ride. Lucky nestled beside Jack. He listened as she chattered her apology, saying that she'd seen a footprint of what might have been a cougar until she decided it was nothing more than an imprint from a big dog. Her words swirled around him; he listened with only half his mind.

So what if she hadn't obeyed his folks? he asked himself. Lots of kids blew off adults, even if he and Ashley didn't. Besides, Jack knew Lucky didn't understand why walking on a burn area was so bad. His dad had once explained that scorched soil was extra fragile and that feet walking on it caused it to erode—to the point that it could even trigger a mud slide. But his dad had taught them that long before Lucky showed up at their home. So how could she know?

When Ashley finally spoke, it was to ask how much farther they had to drive. "Hold out for a few more miles," Olivia answered. "Park headquarters is at the end of this road. That's where I need to go." Olivia looked at her watch. "It's already nearly four o'clock, so the people at headquarters won't be there too much longer. The rest of you might want to hike down to Spruce Tree House. It's the cliff dwelling nearest to headquarters."

After they left the rental car in the parking lot, Steven, Ashley, Jack, and Lucky began winding down the asphalt trail that led to Spruce Tree House. Enough foliage grew close by that they couldn't get a clear view of the 800-year-old dwellings as they walked, although Jack strained for a look around every bend.

"Just a second," Ashley said, taking hold of Lucky's arm. "I want to talk to you."

Lucky frowned. "What about?"

"Just...just...about something," Ashley answered. Then, to Jack, she said, "You and Dad go on ahead. We won't be long."

Enough other visitors crowded the trail that Ashley and Lucky soon got separated from Jack and Steven. Jack looked back, peering around the clumps of tourists, trying to see what was going on between the two girls. Ashley kept clutching Lucky's arm, while Lucky tried to jerk away. At first Lucky seemed to be protesting apologetically, then she looked angry. Jack was about to run back to them, but his father grabbed his shoulder. "Let them alone," he said. "Whatever it is between them, they can settle it themselves."

A park ranger named John was talking to a group of tourists at a bend in the trail; Steven decided it was a good spot to wait for the girls.

"This seep spring is where the inhabitants of Spruce Tree House got their water," John said. "It's still a source of water for the animals in the park. Lots of mornings you can see their tracks and their scat—deer, coyotes, even bears and cougars."

"What is scat?" a woman asked.

"Animal droppings. They're pretty distinctive."

Backing up, the woman examined her shoes. With a mischievous grin, John said, "Yeah, you know what the park rules are—don't pick up anything and carry it out of the park."

That was pretty funny. Laughing at the ranger's joke, Jack didn't notice that Ashley and Lucky were catching up to the group until he heard Ashley say accusingly, "You took something from the burn area. Why don't you just admit it?"

"Hey—what does it hurt if I took one little blue flower?" Lucky shrugged and flashed Jack a crooked smile, as if to say, "Your sister's weird."

"It wasn't a flower!" Ashley insisted. "I saw you dig up something."

"Don't be stupid, Ashley."

"Come on you two, knock it off," Jack interrupted. "The ranger was talking—"

"It was small and blue," Ashley went on, ignoring Jack.

"Right. A flower. Look." Lucky thrust out her hand to show them a withering, pale blue blossom.

"No, something else. You pulled it *out* of the ground. Whatever it was, you better turn it over to the ranger."

Lucky's words came out hard and cold. "You're a liar!"

Frowning, the ranger named John stopped talking and focused his attention on the two girls.

Lucky's eyes darted from Ashley to Jack, then to the ranger and back to Jack again. "You're crazy!" she shouted. "I didn't take anything! Leave me alone!" Spinning on the tips of her sandals, she began to race up the trail.

"Lucky, wait!" Steven cried.

Her auburn hair flew out behind her like a flag as she ran faster and faster, until she disappeared behind a bend.

The ranger raised his eyebrows. "Did she really take something from the park? That's serious."

"A wildflower!" Jack shouted. "No big deal!"

He began to hurry after Lucky. Steven followed Jack, but Ashley was far ahead of them. When they reached the ledge where the cliff dwellings stood, Ashley was already there, and Lucky was screaming at her, "You think I stole something? Fine. Go ahead and search me!"

"Lucky, calm down," Steven commanded. "We can handle this without theatrics."

Arms out, she stood before Steven, crying, "I can tell you don't believe me. Go ahead! Search me."

Steven recoiled. The tourists on the ledge stared at Lucky, wondering what was happening with this girl who seemed to be out of control.

Jack moved protectively toward Lucky, but Ashley pushed ahead of him, saying, "OK, if everyone else is afraid to, I'll search her."

"Go on, put your hands in my pockets," Lucky insisted, and Ashley did. Next, Ashley dropped to her knees, slapping Lucky's legs, harder than she needed to, Jack thought.

"Here, check the cuffs of my socks. I might have shoved something down there. Right?" Lucky sneered. "How about my shirt? Anything there? Wait, you forgot my hair. Or how about my shoes? Maybe I put it in one of them."

Ashley just shook her head. "There's nothing."

Lucky's smile was triumphant.

CHAPTER FIVE

Maybe a lot of people freaked out up there on those ledges, because a woman ranger who was standing near the cliff dwellings seemed to know just how to handle Lucky's stormy outburst. Gently coaxing the girl to come forward, the woman said, "The Ancestral Puebloans were a peaceful people, and I believe their spirits are in this place. Can you feel them?"

"No," Lucky said.

"Me either," Ashley muttered.

"Stop and listen. The people led a gentle life, hunting and gathering from the land. May I tell you how they lived?"

When the two girls nodded, the woman ranger moved closer to Lucky. "You'll be interested in this, I think. How old are you? Fourteen? Fifteen?"

Lucky shook her head. "Thirteen."

"Thirteen? And you?" she asked Ashley.

"Almost eleven."

"Still young. See these?" She pointed to large stones on the ground. "Know what they are?"

Lucky shrugged. "Rocks. Big and little ones."

"Uh-huh. They're metates and manos for grinding corn. The ancient people made cornmeal that way, and guess what? Even today, Hopi women like me still use the mano and the metate for special ceremonies. Some of us are descendants of the Ancient Puebloans who lived right here in Mesa Verde. Today, many Hopi people live on mesa tops in northern Arizona, in homes that look very much like the ones you see here."

Jack began to relax a little as the soft voice of the Hopi ranger worked like magic on Lucky, calming her. "Why don't you kneel down," the woman asked Lucky, "and put your hands on the small stone? That's a mano. Imagine there are kernels of corn under it between the mano and the metate, and you have to grind the corn real fine."

A small crowd had begun to gather around the ranger. Jack glanced at the metal name tag pinned onto her shirt: Nancy Lomayaktewa. Nancy's black eyebrows curved in high semicircles above her warm, dark eyes; she had a stillness about her that seemed to fit the tranquillity of the dwellings.

"When I was a little older than you," Nancy began, talking mainly to Lucky, "my grandmother came to get me one day at my mother's home. My mother already had me dressed up in traditional Hopi clothing, with my hair fixed in the squash blossom. That means it was tied up high on both sides. In the museum up there"—she pointed to the top of the hill—"you can see pictures of the squash blossom hairdo because here in Mesa Verde, 800 or 900 years ago, the women wore their hair just that way."

Nancy took Lucky's thick auburn hair in her hands and lifted it, curving it high. Some of the tension seemed to melt out of Lucky's body as she leaned back against Nancy's touch, as she let herself be soothed by the woman's voice. "When you're a young Hopi girl," Nancy went on, "when you're not married, your hair's always supposed to be fixed like that. But when you're married in the Hopi way, your hairstyle changes."

It was quiet on the ledge except for the raucous calling of a pair of Steller's jays. The deep blue of their outstretched wings stood out against the paler blue of the sky. "Go on, please," Lucky said.

"For the puberty ceremony there's a little house built for you inside your grandmother's or your aunt's home—in a corner, or in a living room or a bedroom. It's covered with heavy canvas because for four days you're not allowed to see the sun."

Closing her eyes, Lucky murmured, "I wouldn't like that. I don't like the dark."

"Well, when you're in the little house, the only time you're allowed to come out is after the sun goes down.

You're not allowed to wash your face or fix your hair, and by about the third day the hairdo's starting to fall down. The only food you can eat is fresh fruit, fresh vegetables, and water. No salt, no fat because you're cleansing yourself."

Bending over the metate, Lucky tentatively pushed the mano along the sloping rock slab.

"Yes, just like that," Nancy said. "You stay there in the little house for three days, kneeling like you're doing right now, grinding corn all day. Your relatives will bring in whole kernels of corn, either blue or white," Nancy continued, holding out her hands as if bearing a gift. "Four grinding stones are set up for you— one really big stone, then each one after that smaller— and you just keep grinding the corn again and again to make it into flour."

Lucky looked up with faraway eyes. Now Nancy's voice took on a faraway sound, too, as if she'd gone back inside her memory to relive the time and place of her special ceremony.

"On your final day, the fourth day, you get awakened early in the morning, before sunrise. That's when all your relatives come. They take down your hair and wash it in warm water, using the root of the yucca plant for shampoo. Then they give you your Hopi naming, from your clan, and they give you many gifts—things you'll need for your life. And then, when that's done, your aunt or your grandmother who's putting you through the ceremony will take you to the edge of the mesa and will have you greet the sun that's just rising."

The woman gestured toward the sun. Now, in late afternoon, it was setting, slanting long rays toward them to light the ancient stone dwellings with a golden glow. "When you see the sun rising early in the morning, you only see the forehead of it. That's my Sun clan. The Sun Forehead. My aunt gave me my Hopi name: White Spider Girl."

Lucky's eyes glittered with tears. "I don't have any grandmother or aunts," she said. "Or anybody, really."

Jack noticed Ashley frowning and biting her lip. He could read his sister, and he knew she was feeling bad about the scene she'd caused with Lucky, who, after all, had no mother to love her. Since he was still mad at Ashley, Jack didn't want to hear any apologies from her, not right then; at least not until he'd had a chance to really ream her out for acting so nasty and suspicious toward Lucky. "Is there more?" he asked, wanting to keep Nancy talking before Ashley had a chance to butt in.

"Yes. After greeting the sun you do your praying, then they take you back to your home, and that's when all the good food is made. They teach you how to make the traditional piki bread that's cooked on rocks over an open fire. Piki bread comes from blue corn that's grown by the Hopi people. When you get back, they fix your hair into the squash blossom. Then they cut your sideburns, representing to your people that you've gone through the puberty ceremony." Nancy smiled, bobbed her head a little, and said, "That's it!"

All the park visitors who'd gathered around to hear the story burst into applause. Nancy took Lucky's hand and helped her to her feet; to Jack's surprise, Lucky leaned forward to give the ranger a hug. More than a hug—for a long moment, Lucky clung to Nancy's comforting figure.

Since peace seemed to have been restored, Steven announced, "I'm going back up to take some pictures while the sunlight's flooding the dwellings this way."

"Yes, the sun's good right now," Nancy agreed. "The best place for picture taking is on the back porch of the chief ranger's office."

"Thanks," Steven said. "You kids want to come with me? If you don't, you can stay here a little longer. Meet me up above when you're ready."

"OK, Dad. Later," Jack said. This gave him the chance, for the first time since they had arrived at these ancient dwellings, to really look around at Spruce Tree House. Situated on a ledge with a wide rock overhang above it, the settlement was the exact color of the surrounding rock.

Nancy had turned her attention to another group of visitors. He heard her telling them that Spruce Tree House was the third largest cliff dwelling in the park, with 114 rooms and 8 kivas, which were small chambers dug into the earth with their roofs at ground level. Kivas were used for ceremonial as well as domestic functions, Nancy was saying; the beamed roofs had collapsed on most of the kivas, but one had been restored and could only be entered by a ladder. She told the group to be sure to look at the hearth in the center of the kiva's floor, as well as at the ventilator shaft on the south side. As Jack climbed down into the gloom of that kiva, he tried to concentrate on where he was, but it was difficult. He was still so mad at Ashley, he found it hard to focus.

Looking around in the dimness of the kiva, he thought how hard it would have been to stay in such a small space during the cold winter months. The base of the ladder rested near a firepit sunk into the floor. It looked as though the Ancestral Puebloans had a choice of either choking from smoke or letting the smoke waft up through the opening above, where the cold air would pour in.

When he climbed back up the ladder, he found Lucky waiting for him. Ashley came up to them and asked, "Are you ready to go?"

"Not with you," Jack replied harshly. "I don't even want you around me after what you did."

"Honest, Jack—"

"Don't start! Just leave us alone."

Ashley stared miserably from her brother to Lucky. "Come on," Jack said, taking Lucky's hand. "Let's climb." He didn't even glance back to see if Ashley was following them up the switchback trail toward the museum and the other park buildings at the top. As far as he was concerned, she could stay down on the ledge all night.

At the chief ranger's office, Steven had started packing his camera equipment while Olivia stood waiting. "Let's grab some dinner at the restaurant," she said, "and after we're finished, we can move our things into the place where we'll be staying. You'll love it! It used to be a water tower. It's round, kind of like a medieval castle."

Jack wasn't sure whether his father had told his mother about Ashley accusing Lucky at Spruce Tree House; about the big, embarrassing outburst. Probably he had, because Olivia didn't ask Jack where his sister was. Anyway, from their vantage point on the chief ranger's porch, they could see Ashley straggling up the trail, looking forlorn, and pouring her heart out to Nancy Lomayaktewa. The role of Mother Comforter seemed to have been thrust on Nancy that afternoon.

All through dinner in the nearby restaurant Jack kept his face turned away from Ashley, while Olivia tried unsuccessfully to smooth things between them. Finally, she mentioned softly, confidentially, "Jack and Ashley, I think I've got a pretty big problem. I went and examined the cougar the rangers caught."

Jack nodded. "The one that hurt the little boy?"

"What did you find out?" Ashley asked eagerly. "Did it have rabies or something?"

Olivia glanced around, checking whether anyone at any of the tables nearby might be listening before she answered. "From what I can tell, it appears to be disease free, which is what I expected. The cat is a young, healthy male, about two years old, in excellent condition. I looked over the results of the blood tests. I examined him. Every test that I could think of that could possibly explain deviant behavior came back negative." Brows furrowing together, she told them, "This is definitely *not* the profile of a cougar that would attack a human."

"So? What are you thinking?" Steven asked.

"I think they may have trapped the wrong cat."

Ashley's eyes grew wide. "The wrong one! So, the real attack cat is still out there, loose?"

"Shhh," Olivia warned.

"Why should I be quiet?"

Olivia leaned closer and dropped her voice to a near whisper. "Because the park prefers that we don't talk too much about it until I've had a chance to investigate more. The circumstances are too strange. Cougars are nocturnal, you know—they usually hunt only at night. This attack happened in broad daylight. Normally, cougars stay as far away from people as possible unless they're caught by surprise. Not this time. The little boy was with his family—parents, two brothers, and grandparents."

"Did his brothers run away and desert him?" Ashley asked, staring pointedly at Jack.

"Actually," Olivia answered, "the brothers saved his life. Both of them chased after the cougar. It had the little boy in its mouth and was carrying him off, which slowed it down enough that the brothers were able to catch up to it and scare it. But before the cougar dropped the child, it gave him some pretty nasty bites on his ear and on one cheek."

Lucky raised her hand to her own cheek, touching it lightly, shuddering.

"Also, getting back to the animal in the cage, when I examined its scat, I found it full of deer hair. That means the cougar had been feeding just a short while before it supposedly attacked. With a full stomach, it would have had no reason to go searching for another meal. So, why would it have gone after a small child?"

"I don't know. Why?" Steven asked.

"Because maybe the cougar in the cage isn't the cougar that hurt the child. That's why, before we go back to the round house, I've got to call park head-quarters and tell them my theory—that they may have trapped the wrong animal."

After they left the restaurant and while Olivia made her call from a pay phone, the rest of them pulled their luggage from the trunk of the car. As they carried it into the round house, Lucky exclaimed, "This is so cool! It really does look like a castle. I love the circular staircase."

Clambering down the twisting adobe stairs, Steven commented, "Pretty small castle! I checked—there's only one bedroom upstairs, with only one bed: a double. Olivia, how 'bout if you and I use the pull-out sofa down here in the living room? We'll put Ashley and Lucky in the double bed, and Jack can sleep in the sleeping bag on the floor."

"Here?" Jack asked. "In the living room?"

"Sorry, son, there's not enough room down here," Steven told him. "With the sofa bed pulled out, your mom and I will barely be able to walk to the kitchen or the bathroom. But there's another room upstairs—well, it's more like a closet. It's empty, and it's big enough— just barely—for you to roll out your sleeping bag."

"Does it have a door?" Jack asked.

"Yes, but no window, so it might get a bit stuffy in there. But it's just for two nights, and it ought to be cool enough after the sun goes down."

"OK," Jack said. He wouldn't mind being on the upper level with the girls as long as he could have some privacy.

"I don't know how much hot water there's going to be for showers," Olivia announced. "Who wants to go first?"

"I will," Lucky said. "Let me just get a few things out of my duffel." She unzipped the canvas bag to pull out clean clothes. Jack was no expert, but it seemed to him that Lucky's things looked expensive. The shirt was designer—he could see the label. The jeans were brand name, too.

"I'll carry Lucky's tote upstairs," Ashley volunteered, trying to make amends, Jack supposed.

The round house was so small they could hear Lucky turn on the shower. She started humming, then she sang out, *"Near, far, wherever you are, I believe that the heart does go on...."*

Steven chuckled, "She's a good-looking girl, but she sings off key." Olivia giggled at that, but Jack glowered. He was still scowling when he looked up to see Ashley coming down the stairs, slowly, quietly, one step at a time, holding a small square of paper in her fingers.

"Look at this," she said, handing it to Olivia.

"What? Numbers. Wait—this is my telephone credit card number. Whose handwriting is this?"

Tossing her head, Ashley gestured toward the bathroom, where Lucky's singing had grown even louder, *"You're here, there's nothing to fear...."*

"How did she get my phone card number?" Olivia wondered. Her brows knit together as she looked at Steven questioningly.

"I know," Ashley answered. "When you made that phone call in the Denver airport, Lucky was standing real close behind you, watching you dial."

"And she wrote down the number?"

Shaking her head, Ashley said, "She must have memorized it."

Steven glanced at the paper. Sounding incredulous, he exclaimed, "Fourteen digits? She could memorize fourteen digits without writing them down? Uh-uh, I don't think so. Anyway, where did you get this?"

Ashley flushed bright red. "I—found it."

Pulling himself up to his full five-foot-six-inch height, Jack asked menacingly, *"Found* it? Where?"

Ashley stammered, "Her tote bag was open."

"You went through her things!" Jack's fists clenched. He felt like decking his little sister.

"I saw her pick up something from the burn area! I saw it, whether you believe me or not. She had to hide it *somewhere!* I was trying to find it."

"Ashley, I'm ashamed of you," Olivia declared. "It's not right to go through someone else's personal property. Don't you ever do anything like that again. Now give me that piece of paper. Your father and I need to discuss this problem alone."

"But Mom—"

"I said now!"

Ashley handed over the paper, then burst into tears and ran up the steps.

"...and my heart will go on and on," Lucky sang from the shower.

CHAPTER SIX

They ate breakfast in the same restaurant where they'd had dinner the night before, since the next nearest restaurant was six miles back along the park road. The tables were small squares, which made it hard to ignore someone who was only three feet away, but Jack and Ashley still were not speaking to each other. Jack pored over a map of the park, while Ashley, eyes glued to her lap, twisted a napkin into a string.

"What's everyone going to do today?" Olivia asked brightly. "I've got a meeting concerning the cougar right after I finish here. As you can imagine, the rangers weren't very happy when I told them I believed they caught the wrong cat. We're going to try to make a game plan on how to search out the real one, which means"— she took a sip of coffee— "you'd better plan the day without me."

Steven answered, "I want to photograph Cliff Palace.

It's the largest cliff dwelling in the park. It's got some intact rooms, and in a few places there are interesting designs painted on the inside walls. I should be able to get some great shots."

"That sounds good, Dad," Ashley said. "Cliff Palace is the most famous place here. I can't wait to see it."

Jack looked up from the map. "Fine. Drop us off at Balcony House."

Steven asked, "Drop who off?"

"Lucky and me." Eyes lowered, Jack tried to fold the map back into its original shape, but like all maps, it resisted. "Balcony House is just down the road from Cliff Palace. You and Ashley go on and get your pictures, Dad. I'll be at Balcony House with Lucky."

"We can all start at Balcony House. I wanted to get some shots there too—" Steven began.

Jack looked up abruptly. "You can take your own pictures when you come to pick us up. Lucky and I want to go alone."

"I think that's a tour where kids have to be accompanied by an adult, Jack," Olivia said gently.

"Couldn't you just call one of the rangers you know and ask if the person giving the tour can be in charge of us? I mean, it's not like we're little kids or anything, and you're busy working on park business so that almost makes you an employee of Mesa Verde"—Jack took a breath—"which means they might give us a break and let us go alone."

When his mother hesitated, Jack pressed harder. "We'll stay right with the ranger and do whatever he or she says. Lucky and I really want to go there by ourselves. Please, Mom? It's just one hour."

Steven and Olivia exchanged glances. Olivia nodded, and a wisp of a smile brushed Lucky's lips.

"OK." Steven sighed. "I guess it's settled as long as the ranger agrees to all of this. Ashley, it's just going to be you and me. Hope you won't mind being stuck with the old man."

He'd meant to be funny, but Ashley didn't smile.

The four of them drove in stony silence as the car looped around the road to Balcony House, with Steven and Ashley in the front seat, Jack and Lucky in back. Their hands, resting side by side on the seat, barely touched.

The interpretive ranger who met Jack and Lucky at Balcony House couldn't have been more different from Nancy, the guide at Spruce Tree House. Young and thin, Stan LaPointe seemed as animated as Nancy had been soothing. His small, wire-framed glasses couldn't hide the energy in his blue eyes, and when he told stories, the crowd of people gathered around him punctuated his words with bursts of laughter. Jack knew this was going to be fun, especially since, at Olivia's request, the ranger had agreed to look out for Jack and Lucky.

"Some visitors ask interesting questions," Ranger LaPointe told the people waiting at the starting place for the tour to begin. "They'll say, 'Why did the Puebloans build their cliff dwellings so far from the road?'"

"'Cause there weren't roads way back then," a small boy shouted.

"Very good." Smiling, Stan said, "Maybe you'll grow up to be a ranger one day. How about this one? Sometimes I get asked, 'What did the Ancestral Puebloans use for water?'"

The little boy frowned in concentration until his face suddenly cleared. "That's dumb. They used water for water."

Throwing his hands up to the sky, Stan said, "Exactly right! Man, are you smart. If you keep this up, I might be out of a job. These folks are going to ask you to run this tour."

Lucky giggled at the exchange, which made Jack relax a little. Since Ashley's accusation, Lucky had been withdrawn, almost cold. It was good to see her face break into its usual bright smile.

"OK. It's ten o'clock. We're just about ready to begin," Stan announced. "I need to go over a few safety rules that are always in effect here but are especially important now because of the cougar problem. Are any of you aware of this?"

A few tourists nodded, but most looked puzzled.

"I don't want to scare you, but you need to know that Mesa Verde has been troubled by an aggressive cougar. A little boy was hurt—"

"Didn't they already catch the one that attacked him?" a woman asked.

"We thought we had, but last night we got some new information that makes us think we may have captured the wrong cougar. There's no cause to panic, though," Stan said, holding up his hands as if he were a traffic cop. "Just follow the basic rules, and everything should be fine. Normally, the cats keep as far away from people as possible. So don't wander from the group, and make sure you stay on the established trails. Any questions?"

"Why don't you just eliminate the problem?" a man in a dusty pair of Levis asked. "Seems like the park's putting a lot of good folks in danger. Give me a rifle and about two days, and I guarantee you won't be looking into the mouth of any cougar."

Stan colored. "Every animal has the right to be here," he began. "We're trying to find the problem cat and get that particular animal out of the park. The rest of the cougars are necessary for keeping the ecological balance, meaning that if you take one link out of the natural chain, the entire chain becomes weak. We definitely need to keep the cougars here."

The man in the Levis rubbed his hand against his sweaty forehead. "So, in the meantime you're just gonna let people get chewed up till you get around to catching the right one?"

Jack shook his head and murmured to Lucky, "Listen to that guy. I wish my mom was here to take him on."

"We're doing all we can," Stan assured him. "We realize that a lot of people have traveled halfway around the world to see Mesa Verde. Would you want us to shut down the park and keep them from seeing it?"

A chorus of "No, no!" rang in the air.

"So the best we can do is to be careful and then enjoy the incredible beauty of this park." Stan turned his attention once again to Balcony House. "The place we are going to is really very special. Archaeologists once thought that Balcony House was a family dwelling. Now we believe that's not true. It appears to have been a place of spiritual worship. So please, treat it as you'd like others to treat your own church. Don't touch anything, or sit on the walls, or act disrespectfully here. Are you ready to go and have a great time?"

Forty-two heads, including Jack's and Lucky's, nodded yes.

Stan led them down a narrow path that skimmed the edge of the cliffs until everyone bottlenecked at a gate. "The point of no return," Stan joked, unlocking the gate with a key. While they handed him their tickets for the tour, he kept up a steady stream of information about the park. "The Whetherill brothers named this canyon Soda Canyon. Does anyone know why?"

When no one could answer, Stan pushed his ranger hat to the back of his head, hooked his thumbs in his belt, and drawled, "It's because the brothers looked out over this canyon—the biggest one in the park—and said, 'Well, golly, that there canyon's so'da wide and so'da deep, ain't it?'" Stan grinned as the crowd moaned. "But seriously," he added, locking the gate behind the crowd, "it's because there's all this white deposit around here. The settlers thought it was baking soda, but it's not. It's actually calcium carbonate. The canyon was named before they figured that out."

"Why is he locking us in?" Lucky whispered.

Overhearing her question, Stan answered, "This cliff dwelling requires our visitors to do a lot of climbing on some pretty tall ladders. We have to make sure a guide is present at all times, for visitor safety as well as for the protection of Balcony House. Now, if any of you get truly terrified, you'll have an option: You can hike back here and wait at the gate for the next ranger to let you out."

"Ladders?" Lucky asked. "Jack, you didn't say anything about climbing a ladder."

"Sorry. I didn't know. Maybe that's why you're supposed to go with an adult."

Lucky paled. "I don't like being locked in. And I don't like heights." She gripped the top of his arm, digging her nails into his skin like tiny claws. "Come on, let's go back."

Stan was already ahead of them, chatting as he hurried to catch up to the rest of the group, telling about the canyon wall's unique water filtration system. The people had gathered six deep around an alcove.

Stan began to explain how the Puebloans might have collected several gallons of water each day from the small seep spring.

"Come on, Lucky, we'll be OK," Jack told her. "I'll help you. Besides, if you back out now, we'll have to be with Ashley."

"But—"

"It's a ladder!" Jack exclaimed, wearing his most confident smile, "How bad can it be?"

Later, when he stared at the double-wide wood rungs that seemed to stretch forever up the sheer cliff wall, he felt his insides quiver. He'd climbed steep places before, but never when the drop beneath him was so sharp, so certain to bring death. He envisioned himself slipping, bouncing off the alcove and then tumbling down into the deep canyon beneath. How had the Ancestral Puebloans managed? How would Lucky?

"Now *that's* a ladder," he said, trying to laugh.

"This isn't funny. Why did you bring me here?" she hissed in his ear. "Look at that thing—it's a hundred feet tall! I can't do it! No way!"

Jack shook his head. If they returned to the gate to wait for another ranger, he'd have to face Ashley's smug expression when she learned about it. No, he wouldn't go back, which meant there was only one way out. Up. "We'll just have to do it," he told Lucky.

"...and for those of you who don't know how to climb a ladder, I will demonstrate," Stan said cheerily.

With his back to the rungs, he crept up, facing the deep chasm below. "Only joking, folks. You do it like this." Flipping around, he faced the rungs. "Foot, hand, foot, hand." As easily as a spider monkey, Stan scaled the double-wide ladder until he reached the very top. "The ladder shakes slightly, especially when you get to the middle. I'll be waiting for you up here. Start going, two at a time."

The tourists, many looking nervous, began to move up the ladder. A thin man, eyes wide, shook his head and said something in German to the man on his left. Jack decided that Lucky must not be the only one scared to go up. She hung back until all the others had reached the top. A group of them looked down the ladder at Jack and Lucky, waiting.

"Come on," Stan yelled. "The trick is to not look down."

"It's show time," Jack said, trying to keep his voice light. "I'll be right beside you."

At first, Lucky mounted the ladder almost as easily as Jack did. Hand, foot, hand, foot, hand, foot—the rhythm kept his mind focused. Every few rungs he looked over at Lucky, who gripped the rungs so tightly her knuckles jutted white but kept moving steadily.

"You're both doing great," Stan called down.

"I really hate this," Lucky called back. A ripple of laughter went through the cluster of tourists who waited at the top.

They'd made it three-quarters of the way up when Lucky froze. Jack could hear her breathing become rapid, as if she were panting. "You're shaking the ladder!" she shrieked. "It's moving."

"No, it's OK. I won't move," Jack promised. "You go on up."

It seemed to take all of Lucky's effort to advance one hand. Then another foot. "It moved again!" she cried. "Why is it doing that?"

"I'll come down—" Stan began.

Jack had never seen Lucky's eyes as wide as they were now. "No!" she screamed. "Stay there. You'll shake the ladder even more!"

"OK, OK," Stan called. "Don't panic. Everything's going to be fine. Would you rather back down and walk back to the gate?"

Ignoring Stan, Lucky kept her head down. "Jack! Help me! I'm going to fall!"

The people at the top had quieted down, realizing for the first time how terrified Lucky was. Instinctively, Jack knew he had to keep her calm, to coax her like the baby animals his mother sometimes brought home to nurse.

"Lucky, listen, there's nothing to be afraid of."

"How about dying!"

"You're not going to fall. I promise, you're not."

"I can't do it." Her forehead was pressed into a rung. Jack could see her legs shaking.

"Just look straight ahead and take a deep breath. Take all the time you need."

"I can't move!"

Jack noticed that her skin was turning white, and the trembling had moved up to her hands. Stan seemed to sense it was best to let Jack try coaxing her through, at least for the moment. He stood poised at the top of the ladder, waiting for a signal from Jack before he intervened.

"You have to do something for me, Lucky," Jack went on. "You have to stop looking down." When she raised her chin, he said, "Good. Now I want you to imagine that there's land right underneath you, OK? It's just no big deal. You're only a foot off the ground right now."

"I...I'm trying."

"Don't think about anything else but the next rung. Move just one rung up, OK? That's all I'm going to ask you to do."

Slowly, Lucky let go of one hand. With all her strength, she grabbed the rung above. Then the next hand, followed by one foot, then the other.

"You're doing great. All right!" Jack cried. "You're going to leave me down here, feeling stupid."

"I don't think so." Lucky's voice wavered, but the tiniest smile curled a corner of her mouth.

"One more rung with your foot," Jack coaxed. Hesitantly, Lucky moved her foot, and Jack followed, reassuring, cajoling until she grasped the metal hand-holds at the top and Stan pulled her to safety. "Way to go," he told her, as the remaining crowd burst into applause. "You made it!"

Jack clambered over the top just as Lucky answered Stan, "Thanks to Jack. He saved me."

Lucky was babbling. Information spilled out of her mouth in a waterfall of words, with Olivia, Steven, and Jack drinking it in.

Only Ashley seemed apart, even though they all shared the same small, square table at the Spruce Tree Restaurant. Ashley's eyes roamed the ceiling as Lucky filled in the details of her exciting day. "And then Stan, the ranger, said that there might be spirits in Balcony House and that at times he's even felt like he was intruding up there because it's a sacred place," Lucky said eagerly. "So I tried to feel their presence, but I didn't sense anything. And right then, this hawk flies by and just soars right in front of me! I couldn't believe it! Maybe the ancient spirits were sending me some kind of message."

Jack continued, "After Lucky was so scared on that ladder, I was sure we'd be in big trouble when she saw the rest of Balcony House. The first courtyard had a wall, but the second—" He made a slicing motion with his hand. "No barrier, just straight down to the canyon floor. If you fall, splat!"

Nodding, Lucky flashed Jack a smile. "But, with Jack beside me, I was OK. Stan showed us these two kivas with sipapus in them. A sipapu is a hole in the bottom of the kiva. Stan said the People believed their ancestors once came through a hole to Earth—that their spirits traveled up through four levels, from the lower worlds all the way into this one. That's what the sipapu symbolizes."

When Lucky took a breath, Ashley broke into the conversation. "You should have seen Cliff Palace. Dad and I—"

Without waiting for Ashley to finish, Jack talked right over the top of her. This was Lucky's story, not Ashley's. Maybe now his sister would get the point: Being nasty to Lucky was the same as being nasty to Jack.

"I'm telling you, you guys should have seen Lucky!" Jack said loudly, keeping his eyes focused on his parents. "I mean, there she was, afraid of heights, and we were, like, floating right over the edge of this humongous canyon, and instead of being scared, she really got into what the ranger said about the Ancestral Puebloans. And right at the end of the tour was this tunnel we had to crawl through to get out of Balcony House. You had to leave a different way than you went in."

"Yeah. It was this little, tiny tunnel, about this big." Lucky made her arms into a square. "I was afraid the lady in front of me was going to get stuck, but finally she squeezed through." Lucky began to laugh, her eyes dancing as she thought of the woman. "And then those other steps on the way out! I thought the first ladder was bad! There are these toeholds carved into the sides of the sandstone walls. They go straight up the cliff, and that's how you have to get up, putting your toes into them, one foot after the other."

"I thought you were going to freak out again—"

"But I didn't because you were right there behind me—"

"I would have caught you if you fell—"

This time, Ashley's voice exploded like a cannon. *"Dad and I had fun at Cliff Palace!"*

The whole table fell silent. Ashley looked around, color rising in her cheeks. "We did! I helped him take pictures. It was really big, and our ranger said that it was the biggest and the most important cliff dwelling in all of Mesa Verde!"

"You were a great help, Ashley," Steven agreed, patting her shoulder. "I couldn't have taken all those pictures without you."

More silence. Even though his conscience stabbed at him, Jack set his jaw firmly. Ashley was getting what was coming to her. Just to teach her a lesson, he'd keep shutting her out of the conversation. "I learned a lot about the Ancestral Puebloans at Balcony House," he said to his parents. "That's what I'm going to write my paper on for school. Did you know Mesa Verde is the only national park specially set aside to preserve the work of prehistoric people?"

"True," Olivia said, "but in addition to that, it's a great

place to be an animal. Speaking of which, I'd like to tell you about *my* day—"

A shrill series of beeps cut into Olivia's sentence. Looking down to the small, black box on her belt, she sighed and said, "Sorry, I'm being paged by the park. Did I show you guys this pager they gave me? It's so they can find me at all times. I feel like a doctor on call." Craning her neck around the room she asked, "Does anyone know where a phone is?"

"There's one in the gift shop," Ashley told her.

"Great. You all go on and eat. I'll be right back." Scraping her chair against the tile, Olivia hurried to the counter inside the small store that was next to the restaurant. Jack watched his father put his large hand on top of Ashley's small one; she laid her forehead on his hand and closed her eyes.

"Tired, sweetie?" he asked her.

She nodded, then shook her head. "No, not really tired. I'm—"

"I wonder why they're paging Mrs. Landon," Lucky broke in, ignoring Ashley. She picked at squares of lettuce with her fork but didn't eat them.

"It could be the local newspeople. They've been trying to reach her to question her about the cougar situation. You know, Lucky, if you stand next to her when she's interviewed, maybe you could be on TV, too."

"You mean, I could be a star?" Lucky gave a little *huh* of laughter. "Forget that!"

"Why? I thought you'd like it. Anyway, here comes Olivia." Steven knit his brows together as he added, "But by the look on her face, I'd say that whatever's going on isn't good."

By then Olivia had reached their table. "We need to go," she told them quickly, quietly. "Get your things and any food you haven't finished. You can eat it back at the round house."

"What happened?" Ashley asked, sitting up. "Is something wrong?"

"An elderly woman....I keep wondering if I should have encouraged them to close the park. I *knew* that wasn't the right cat...."

Jack leaned forward. "What is it, Mom?"

An expression of regret mixed with alarm clouded her face. "There's been another cougar attack. It's even more serious than the last one. This time the woman may die."

CHAPTER SEVEN

Back at the round house Olivia told them, "Apparently the woman was crouching down at one of the trail-heads, tying her shoe. The cougar came out of nowhere. She's hurt pretty bad."

Ashley shuddered. "That's awful."

"I think your dad should come and photograph the scene where the attack took place. Is that OK with you, Steven?"

"Absolutely," Steven agreed.

"The press and TV are already on to this, and now there are threats to shoot all the cougars in the park. Threats not just from here in Colorado, but from all over the Four Corners area—Utah, Arizona, and New Mexico, too. Other people are saying that if the park doesn't act, they'll come here personally and start put-ting out poison." Closing her eyes, Olivia pressed the tips of her fingers into her lids. "This is getting bad.

There's supposed to be a local citizens' meeting to decide what action they want to take on their own. I'd like to be there so I can try to calm things down."

"You should go, Mom," Jack told her.

Steven leaned forward, resting his elbows on his knees. He searched the kids' faces. "Can you three make it on your own for a while?"

Smiling, Lucky nodded. Jack felt a fizz of excitement at the thought of some time alone with Lucky. He tried not to sound too eager as he assured his parents that the three of them would be just fine, that they'd stay inside and there'd be no problems at all. Only Ashley looked grim.

"Jack, I'm holding you personally responsible for the three of you. We won't be away more than an hour," Steven said as he packed up his camera equipment. "If there's any problem at all, run over to park head-quarters and page Mom on her beeper."

"Not to worry, Dad," Jack assured him, and then Olivia grabbed her briefcase and they were gone. Now if Jack could just get rid of his little sister! In his head he thought of a dozen excuses for asking her to leave— like suggesting she go upstairs and read one of the books she'd brought—but they all sounded so lame that he knew Ashley would make a big deal of them, would refuse to go, and would report everything he said to their parents when they got back. So Jack stayed silent, Ashley hung around, and finally Lucky yawned and said she thought she'd get ready for bed.

A few minutes later Ashley started rattling the door-knob of the tiny bathroom.

"Don't go in there," Jack ordered. "Lucky's in the shower." Lucky had said she needed to wash the sweat from Balcony House out of her hair.

"I just have to brush my teeth," Ashley said. "I'll be in and out in a couple of seconds. She won't even know I'm there."

"OK. Make it fast."

"What makes you the gatekeeper—?" Ashley began, then said, "Oh, never mind." She opened the bathroom door and closed it behind her.

Jack turned his camera in his hands, gently blowing a tiny speck of lint off the lens. Earlier in the day, after they'd safely climbed the toeholds in the rock cliff from Balcony House to the rim above, Jack had asked Lucky if he could take her picture.

She'd shaken her head. "I don't like having my picture taken."

"Why not?"

"I just...don't," she'd answered. "But since you saved my life today, I'll let you take my picture before we leave Mesa Verde."

"When?"

"I don't know. Sometime."

"Tomorrow? Like in the morning?"

Lucky had given him a small smile. "Maybe," she'd told him. "I'll think about it."

He'd had to be content with that. Now he was checking his camera to make sure everything was right—film loaded, batteries strong, lens spotless.

Just then Ashley came out of the bathroom looking puzzled. With her hand outstretched, she walked toward Jack. "I know you're not talking to me, even though what happened was not my fault and you're believing Lucky over me, which makes me feel pretty bad—"

"Knock it off, Ashley—" Jack began.

"But you can still look at this 'cause I think if you do, you'll have to see that there's something really strange about Lucky."

Jack wanted to walk away, but curiosity drew him. "OK. What have you got?"

Ashley opened her hand. "It's Lucky's watch."

"I can see that. So what are you doing with it?" Jack demanded.

"She left it on the glass shelf in the bathroom. I was squeezing the toothpaste when I heard this weird noise. Like a tiny rattle." She hesitated. "First I couldn't figure out what it was, but then I could tell it was coming from the watch, so I thought it was an alarm going off, and I picked it up."

"So?"

"When I picked it up, I couldn't hear the noise anymore, but, Jack, I could *feel* it. It *vibrated!*"

Not understanding, he just stared at her.

"In my hand. I could feel the watch, like, jiggle."

Jack said, "Maybe it's some silent kind of alarm."

"Yeah, but when I looked down at it, I saw these numbers on the dial."

He snorted. "Big surprise! What'd you expect to see? The Energizer Bunny?"

"Listen to me, please! I looked where it's supposed to tell the time. Only it wasn't the time, it was three numbers, then a dash, and then four more. It's a phone number!"

"Let me see," Jack said. When she gave it to him, he said, "I know what this is: It's a pager. You know, like the beeper Mesa Verde gave to Mom? Only this one doesn't beep, it vibrates, so, like, if you're at a concert or something, it won't bother people—you'll just feel it. I saw one advertised in my photography magazine."

"Why does Lucky need a pager?" Ashley asked.

"I don't know. Why do you need to try to nail her all the time?"

He'd just handed the watch back to Ashley when Lucky flung open the bathroom door, her hair hanging in wet ringlets. She had on a white, V-neck nightshirt scattered with tiny red hearts. In two seconds flat her face morphed from good fairy to wicked witch—her eyebrows slammed together in a deep-creased frown, and her lips thinned into a snarl. "What are you doing with my watch?" she shrieked.

Ashley stammered, "N-noth—" but before she got the word out, Lucky had snatched the watch with such force that Ashley reeled backward.

"What is it with you Landons?" Lucky raged, staring at the watch and then quickly buckling it onto her wrist. "I don't mean you, Jack, but everyone else in this family, especially your sister—"

"Wait a second," Jack broke in. "She didn't mean anything. Your watch was making some kind of noise, and she wanted to show me, that's all."

Again, Lucky's face seemed to run through, in split-second succession, a dozen different expressions before she looked up, her eyes filling with tears. She seemed anguished. Pathetic.

"Ashley, why do you hate me so much?" she asked. "What did I ever do to you?"

"I don't hate you," Ashley protested.

Tears began to run freely down Lucky's cheeks. With the palms of her hands, she rubbed them away, leaving fist-size red marks on her skin. "You know, I never had a little sister. I never had anyone in my life that I could really be close to! And when I met you and we sat talking in the living room, I thought you were so cool. I thought we could be special friends. But you've hated me from the start, and I don't even know why."

Vehemently, Ashley declared, "That's not true!"

"Yes, it is. First you accused me of stealing from the burn area, then you went through my duffel bag, trying to find whatever it is you thought I stole—oh yeah, I know about it. Your mom really raked me over the coals on that one. Thanks to you I'll have to deal with Ms.

Lopez about that credit card number, even though I told your folks it's only a number game I play to see how good my memory is. Why didn't you just ask me about it, Ashley? I would have told you."

Ashley's cheeks flamed.

"And now you break into the bathroom and take my watch!"

Keeping her voice even, Ashley explained, "I just went in to brush my teeth, and your watch was making this weird sound, so I picked it up."

"I was scared to death when I looked for it and it wasn't there. You...you took something really precious. This watch is the only thing I have left from...my mom." Lucky's head drooped, as if in painful remembrance. She took a breath. "My mother gave it to me right before she died."

Ashley crossed her arms over her chest.

"I know I'm overreacting, but it's all I've got of my mother. I...I guess I'm too emotional...."

"It's OK—" Jack began. He tried to reach out, but Lucky gently shook his hand off her arm.

"I'm sorry, but right now, I think I need to be alone. I need some space. I'm going for a walk." She went back to the bathroom to retrieve her jeans and a pair of sandals.

"You're leaving? You can't go out at night!" Ashley warned. "There's a crazy cougar out there!"

"I'm not afraid," Lucky said coolly. "The cougar

attacks weren't anywhere around here. They were miles away on the other side of the park, your mother said." Pulling on her jeans, Lucky slipped her feet into her sandals and quickly headed for the door. The nightshirt hung past the knees of her jeans, but she didn't seem to care.

"You're not allowed out alone unless my parents say it's OK," Ashley repeated. "And they're for sure going to say no because the cougar—"

"Would you stop with the cougar? I've handled worse things in my life than a big cat." Lucky's voice turned flinty. "As far as getting your parents' permission, well, they're not here to give it to me, are they? If they come before I get back, you tell them it's your fault that I had to go."

"Leave it alone, Ashley. I'll walk with her," Jack said.

Her face softening, Lucky turned again to look at Jack. "The thing is, I need some time for just me. I won't be long." With that, she breezed out the door.

Jack and Ashley stood silent for a moment, staring at the closed door until Ashley remarked, "What the heck was *that?*"

"What?"

"That. The show. I have never seen anyone throw a fit like she just did. I mean, those tears came out of nowhere. And that story about the watch! Give me a break!"

"She was scared. She thought it was gone."

"No," Ashley said, narrowing her eyes, "that's not what I'm talking about. The whole story about her mom giving it to her right before she died. She was lying. I'm positive she was. And if she was lying about that, could it be that maybe she was lying about taking something from the burn area? Maybe she lies about everything."

A burst of heat erupted inside Jack, created by his own twinge of doubt colliding with the need to stand up for Lucky.

"Think about it," Ashley went on. "Lucky said she was five when her mother died, which means the watch was from eight years ago. You saw that thing—it's brand new. And there's no phone here in the round house, right? So I bet she's on her way to a pay phone to call the number that showed up on her watch." Smiling triumphantly, Ashley finished with, "I say we follow her."

"More spying?" Jack's voice was hot. "You really are out to get her, aren't you?"

For a moment, Ashley didn't answer. It seemed as though his words had hit her hard; she lowered her eyes, then raised them slowly. "So after everything that's happened, you're still taking her side."

"This isn't about sides."

"Yes, it is."

He couldn't meet her gaze. "Look," he said stiffly. "Think what you want. I'm going after her. You stay here and tell Mom and Dad what's going on." When Ashley started to protest, he snapped, "I bet she's right outside, taking in some air. I'll get her and bring her back. End of story."

"Fine." Ashley scowled. "Whatever."

Ashley was angry, but Jack couldn't deal with both his sister and Lucky. Too many emotions crowded inside him; he knew he'd have to deal with them one at a time, starting with Lucky.

Night sounds floated over Jack, and his footsteps crunched beneath him on the path as he searched for Lucky. Wind pushed through scrub pine, sounding strangely like rushing water. Every now and again he heard the hum of a car passing on the road below.

With the moon bright and full, Jack could see clearly enough to know Lucky wasn't anywhere close by. He circled the house once, then again. It was the first time he'd noticed how the house was put together—the square downstairs part built right up against the tall, round tower, with the tower's window looking down on the square roof.

Behind the round house was an old tennis court. Maybe, Jack decided, she'd gone there. He picked his way through the wild grasses until the fence stopped him. Resting his fingers in the chain link, he searched the battered court. Empty.

Almost against his will, he took the trail to the road. Another 200 yards and he'd made his way to the pay phone outside the restaurant.

He could tell it was Lucky by the hair, flaming in a copper halo from the light overhead. Her back was toward him as she feverishly whispered into the phone.

She was making a call, just like Ashley had said. The sight made his chest ache.

At first, Jack thought of returning to the round house without her. He didn't know which he hated more, that his sister was right or that Lucky had lied to him. Still, he waited, uncertain whether to leave or confront her. Suddenly, she snapped the phone back into its receiver and whirled around.

"Jack!" she cried out in surprise. "What are you doing here?"

"You said you just wanted to go for a walk."

"I did. And then I just...." She stumbled, searching for words.

"You got paged on your watch, didn't you? That's why you had to leave. Who'd you call? Who paged you?"

"Maria." Moving confidently toward him, Lucky slid her arm around Jack's and began to pull him in the direction of the round house. "It's good news. She's left the hospital and is back home. I would have told you, but Ashley was standing right there."

"Does Maria live around here?" Jack asked.

"No. Far, far away. Why?"

"You must have had a lot of quarters for the pay phone."

Without the slightest hesitation, Lucky answered, "Oh, I called collect. Maria doesn't care." Then, giving him one of her brilliant smiles, she added, "You know what, Jack? It feels good to talk about it with someone.

I get so tired of secrets. Anyway, Maria said she's OK, but she told me to stay away. It's still too dangerous."

Woodenly, he asked, "Why did you lie about going for a walk?"

She stopped and looked up at him. "I had to make sure Maria was all right, Jack. That's not wrong, is it? Caring about your friends is good."

"Is that watch really from your mom?"

Lucky's face looked pinched. "Why do you want to know? Besides, I thought we were talking about Maria. What's the big deal about my watch?"

From the start, Jack had known Ashley was right about the watch. There were no pager wristwatches eight years ago. It was a brand-new technology; the magazine ad had said so.

"You told me your mom died when you were five." Jack felt sourness in his throat, but he pushed it down and kept going. It was better to get it out in the open and hear the real story, no matter what it turned out to be. "Look, I want you to tell me the truth. It's important to me."

"OK. You want the truth about my watch? The truth is, the pager watch is something I got just a couple of weeks ago, which means my mother, who really, truly is dead, did not give it to me. There, I told you."

Jack shook his head and said, "I don't get it. Why did you tell Ashley that watch was from your mom? Why would you even want to say something like that?"

"I don't know." She shrugged. "It might make her think before she goes through my stuff again. It's a better story—lots of reasons. I'm sorry if that bothers you. I guess you never bend things around, or twist the facts, just a little?"

"No."

"That's good." Lucky nodded, almost as though she were talking to herself. "I guess I've always known that some people were really honest, but, it's not like there's any of that in my life. Maybe you can teach me how."

Jack gazed down at her. What kind of life must she have lived to think that being honest was somehow unique? He was glad she trusted him. It made him want to pull her away from the harsh parts of the world.

They walked the rest of the way to the round house with Lucky hanging on to his arm, apologizing, "These sandals don't work so well on a rocky path." She was small and fine boned; the top of her head came no higher than Jack's ear.

They stopped behind the house. A yellow square marked the upstairs bedroom where Lucky and Ashley had slept last night, although the rest of the house was dark. Ashley must still be awake, and his parents must still be gone.

"It's so nice out here," Lucky said softly. "I don't think I want to go in."

"We'd better, before my dad and mom come back and yell because there's a crazy cougar on the loose, even if it is half a park away. I don't want you to get into trouble."

"What does it matter? Won't Ashley tell on me?"

"I'll ask her not to."

"Wouldn't that be a lie?" Lucky gave a tinkling laugh that sounded like bells.

"OK. You're right. I'll tell the truth and hang you out to dry." He began to move toward the house, but she held him back.

"Wait, before we go inside, I want to look around. You can see everything with this full moon. I mean, it's like a great big headlight's been stuck in the sky. It's lighting up the whole world!"

"Yeah," he said. "Like you can really see this house. It's interesting how they built it with the stones all rough and uneven so they'd look like the old dwellings on the cliffs."

"Uh-huh. But that's not what—"

"I wonder why they made the new part lower than the tower. They could have made it the same height and had a second bedroom," he said, not that he cared. But this moonlit situation was moving in a direction he might not want to follow. A rush of words would hold it back.

"Jack! Forget the house. I wanted to tell you something." Lucky moved closer to him. "It's about me. And you."

He would have loved to hear her say that an hour earlier, but things had changed. Now he felt uneasy about this beautiful but mysterious girl who lied for no reason at all. What stories could she make up if she really had a reason to deceive?

"I don't want you to think that I'm a bad person, because I'm not."

"I...I don't think you're bad."

"Don't lie, Jack, you don't know how. Anyway, what I'm trying to tell you is that even if I stretch the truth sometimes, what I'm going to tell you right now is true." Raising her eyes to his, she said, "I really like you. A lot. I've never met anybody like you before, not in my whole life, and you've made me think about...things. No matter what happens, you can believe that."

She turned her face up to him; later, he would wonder what might have happened if he hadn't, at that moment, heard his parents coming.

"...meeting in an uproar," his mom was saying. From the muted sound of her voice, they were still far down the path. "...screaming for the death of all cougars," she continued. "Of course, they wouldn't listen when I told them this kind of situation was extremely rare. Did you hear them yell at me? They said I should tell that to the latest victim."

"The attack on that woman was not your fault, Olivia."

"Maybe it was!" her voice sounded anguished. "I'm supposed to be the expert. What if I'd advised them to close the park? But that seems like such a huge step...."

Steven answered, "You know that just isn't done, Olivia. When those two women were killed by grizzlies at Glacier National Park, that park wasn't closed. People die in the thermal pools at Yellowstone, and they don't close Yellowstone. Things...happen. It's risky to be in wild places. Visitors accept that because the trade-off is so great—the beauty, the chance to see nature untamed, including the wild animals."

Olivia and Steven were so close now that their words carried clearly in the still night. "Hurry, Jack," Lucky whispered. "We can beat them inside. If we're quick, they won't know we were gone."

Like shadows, they crept into the house through the back door. Silently, they slipped upstairs before the front door rattled open. They'd made it without getting caught.

Jack was learning to break rules. Just like Lucky.

CHAPTER EIGHT

It must be awkward for Ashley, Jack thought, having to share a bed with someone who'd ragged on her, who'd accused her of being nasty and spiteful. Because the tiny closet Jack slept in was uncomfortably stuffy, he'd left the door slightly ajar; if any words had been spoken between the two girls, he would have heard them. Instead, the silence in the round tower bedroom hung heavy with tension.

Ashley hadn't ratted on them to his parents, which was good. It made him almost want to forgive her. But if he did, then what did he really feel about Lucky?

He tried to convince himself that Lucky had told only two real lies—one, about the watch coming from her mother; two, about going for a walk when she really went to make a phone call. But other doubts plagued him, dancing around his head in the dark like tiny grinning goblins.

So only two *real* lies. Then he thought, what about her mother being killed by a white tiger? Another fantasy? Sounded like it. Or could it possibly be true? No, she'd probably invented it because, like she said that evening, it made a good story.

Through his sea of doubts, one stark fact swam up slowly, finally pushing to the surface of his consciousness: When he'd asked Lucky if Maria lived nearby, Lucky had answered that she lived far, far away. But Jack remembered those numbers on the face of the pager watch: three digits, then a dash, then four more digits. No area code! That meant it had to be a local number. Lucky had called someone who was pretty close to the park.

So, lie number three. What about liking him? Was that lie number four, or did she really mean it? Suddenly, he heard her voice. "Ashley," she said very softly, "are you awake?"

"Yes, I'm awake," Ashley answered in her normal voice. "How about you, Jack? Can you hear me from your closet?"

"Uh-huh, I can. What time is it?"

"Must be about midnight. Are you wearing your watch, Lucky?" Ashley asked her.

"Don't start about the watch..." Lucky spat out.

"I'm not! I just—forget it."

Jack could hear the springs squeak as Ashley turned on her side, away from Lucky. Right then he felt sorry for himself and sorry for Ashley, too. He'd been unfair to her.

"I can't sleep," he called out. "Tell us a story, Ashley."

"A story! You mean like a bedtime story?" It was Lucky's voice, sounding scornful.

"My sister's a great storyteller," Jack said. "She knows legends and folktales from all over the world. She reads things and remembers them."

Ashley spoke out, "I have a good one, and it's not from all over the world, it's from right here. Remember when you were mad at me, Jack—"

Which time? he wondered grimly.

"And I walked up the path from Spruce Tree House with Nancy Lomayaktewa? She told me brothers and sisters always get into little squabbles, but it doesn't mean anything because big brothers really love their sisters and try to protect them. Then she told me this story:

In one village on the mesa nothing remained except the beauty—of the sky, of the dwellings set against the cliffs, of the sunrise. Each morning the sun soared up in all its majesty, but when it continued across the heavens, it beat down on the mesa without mercy. There was no rain. Summer after summer, no rain. Without rain no corn could grow for the people to eat. Finally, all the people went away. They fled in many directions, hoping to find a place where there might be food.

In the panic of the great departure, two small children—a brother and a sister—were left behind. They thought surely their parents would come back for them, but one day followed another, and the parents did not return.

The brother searched everywhere for the tiniest morsel of food to give his sister. He found nothing—not a kernel of corn, not a seed from a squash, not even an acorn. At last, to take his sister's mind away from the ache of hunger, he made her a toy. Trimming a dried stalk of sunflower, he cut it into the shape of a hummingbird.

"Spider Woman made all the birds of the air out of clay, and they came to life," he told his sister. "If you toss this toy bird into the air, the breeze will carry it high, and you can pretend it's real."

The girl was delighted with the toy hummingbird. When her brother left to search for food, she threw the little bird into the air again and again. Then, one time it didn't fall back to earth.

Puzzled, the girl watched the bird. It no longer looked like the dried pith of a sunflower stalk. It had feathers that gleamed in the sunlight. Its wings beat so fast they could hardly be seen.

"Spider Woman has made you live!" the girl cried happily. And then, the little bird flew away.

When the brother returned without having found anything to eat, the little girl sat crying. "My bird flew away," she told him. "It came to life, and it flew up to the sky and didn't come back."

The brother thought she must have lost the toy he'd

made her and had invented that story as an excuse. But just then, the little hummingbird fluttered back into sight.

"Oh, did you see him, Brother?" the girl cried. "Did you see him? He has flown into that small space between two stones in our wall. Please bring him back to me."

When the brother stretched his hand inside the niche in the wall, he found not the bird but an ear of ripe corn. It was the first food he'd seen in many days. He hurried to share it with his sister.

Day after day the hummingbird flew away in the morning, flew back at night, and left ripe corn inside the crevice in the stone wall. The brother and sister now had food in abundance.

"Hummingbird, when you fly into the sky each day," the brother begged, "could you search for our parents? If you find them, please bring them back to us." The hummingbird did find the children's mother and father, but they were so weak from hunger they could not make the journey to the village. Heeding the children's pleas, the hummingbird began to take food, each day, to the parents as well as to the children. Soon the mother and father regained their strength, and the family was united once again.

Then the gods allowed the rains to fall. The corn grew green and strong, so that once more there was enough to eat. Before long, the villagers returned to the dwellings set against the cliffs, to the beauty of the sky, the sun, and the mesa.

"And the brother was always kind to his sister, and he didn't get mad at her and yell at her all the time," Ashley added with a tremor in her voice.

"I'm sorry," Jack said softly.

Lucky said nothing.

Maybe because he'd made peace with Ashley, Jack was finally able to fall asleep, although his dreams were disturbing. In one of them Ashley was pounding his shoulder, hitting his face, yelling his name—and he woke up to find her shaking him, trying to wake him.

"What?" he asked, groggy.

"She's gone!"

"Who's gone?" But even half awake, he knew it was Lucky. Clumsily pulling his long legs out of the sleeping bag, he asked, "Where'd she go?"

"Through the window. We've got to tell Mom and Dad."

"No!" He grabbed her hand. "First we'll try to find her ourselves. That way we can talk her back without getting her into trouble."

"I don't know...."

"Please, Ashley! We can do this." As he pulled on jeans and shoes, he thought that Lucky couldn't get very far very fast in those open sandals—*if* that's what she had on.

Ashley grabbed Jack's flannel shirt to throw over her sleep shirt, then turned back to rummage for something else. That let Jack get to the window first. It was a short reach from the window ledge to the square roof below. Even for someone like Lucky who was afraid of heights, it wouldn't have seemed at all scary. Jack eased through the window and dropped as silently as he could, hoping that if his parents heard the noise, they'd think it was squirrels skittering around on the roof. Then he turned and helped Ashley.

"You've got my camera!" he whispered. "Why?"

"No one ever believed me when I said things about Lucky. This time I'm going to take pictures. For proof."

"No, you're not." Jack pulled the camera from her hand. "This is mine, and no one else uses it."

It was no time for an argument, standing there on the roof in the moonlight. "Come on," Jack said. "Over the ledge. It'll be easy."

"Right. Piece of cake."

A small wooden ledge projected beyond the stone wall; Jack hung from it by his hands, then dropped, feet-first, the short distance to the ground. Ashley dug the toes of her tennis shoes into the spaces between the stones, climbing down the cracks like they were toe holes.

They ran to the parking lot, a wide expanse of now empty asphalt. Not too far in the distance, Jack saw a moving flash of white. "There she is!" he cried. "Heading for Spruce Tree House."

"Spruce Tree—?"

"Who knows why? Just get moving before we lose

her." They were already catching only the briefest glimpses of Lucky's white shirt as she moved behind the trees.

"She won't be able to get in there, Jack," Ashley said from right behind him. "There's a gate on that path, and it's locked at night. She can't climb over it 'cause it's got barbed wire."

"Lucky probably doesn't know that. We can catch up while she's figuring out what to do," Jack said.

But when they reached the gate, they didn't find Lucky. Instead, they found a thick blanket draped over the barbed wire that topped the gate and the adjoining fence.

"Look how she made it over!" Ashley exclaimed, shaking her head in admiration. "She must have had it all planned out. Well, if she got over that way, we can too."

"Wait, Ashley, this is getting serious," Jack protested softly. "If we scale the gate, we'll be breaking in. Maybe we really should get Dad."

"No! If we go back now, she'll be gone. We don't have time!"

Reluctantly, Jack agreed. They were violating park rules, maybe even the law, but this was bigger than rules. It took him only a moment to decide: "I'll go first, then I'll help you over."

The chain link rattled when Jack climbed it, bending under his weight as he swung his leg over the top. Thick and rough, the blanket completely protected him from the barbed-wire stingers that edged the top of the fence.

Where had Lucky found that blanket? Jack wondered. He hadn't seen anything like that at the round house.

"Okay, Ashley, give me your hand—"

He needn't have offered. Light and nimble, she scaled the fence like a cat and dropped next to him on the asphalt path.

"I don't get it. Why is she coming in here?" Ashley whispered.

"I don't know."

"If she's running away, you'd think she'd walk on the road. Why Spruce Tree House in the middle of the night?"

"I *said* I don't know!"

"This is crazy."

It was harder now to see. The mountain walls blocked out the moonlight, and the trees dripped deep pools of shadow along the path, black on black. All seemed altered in the half darkness; Jack's footsteps scraped the path like sandpaper while his camera, hanging on its strap, slapped his chest in a hollow drumbeat. "Wait!" he whispered. Holding up his hand, he stopped, listening for any human sound. There was a rustling from a group of scrub oaks to his left. Suddenly, one of the shadows broke free and stood in front of him, blocking his way. Lucky.

"Get—out—of—here!" She bit off every word. It wasn't light enough to make out Lucky's eyes, but Jack didn't need to. He could feel the heat in them, could hear the fury in her voice.

"Lucky—" Jack began.

"Go away!"

Now it was Jack's turn to sound fierce. "Not without you!"

"Forget it!"

"You can't make us leave," Ashley declared. "You might as well come back with us, and then Mom and Dad can—"

"No! Why can't you just *leave me alone?"*

Jack stepped close. Lucky's duffel bag had been slung over her back, like a knapsack. Her hands clutched the straps circling beneath her arms so that her fingers gleamed white.

"Were you going to disappear, just like that, without telling me why? I thought we were friends."

"I'm not going back! I can't!"

"Then you've got a problem," he said evenly. "You won't come with us, and we won't leave. I guess you've got company."

Lucky cursed softly, but Jack held his ground. He had questions for this girl, and he wanted answers. Who was she, anyway? It seemed as though Lucky's personality could change from water into steam and then to ice and right back to liquid in an instant. Which one of those natures was real?

He tried again. "You can run, or you can deal with whatever the problem is. It's your choice."

Seconds ticked by before Lucky answered. "You do

what you have to do, and I'll do what I have to. Good-bye, Jack." Turning, she began to walk down the path, but Jack burst ahead and grabbed her arm. Whirling her around, he looked into her face. He could see enough of it to know her calm voice had been a lie. She was crying.

"Lucky, don't do this. You don't have to run away. Is it the gang? Are you afraid? Stay with us, and we'll work it out."

"Don't you get it, Jack?" It was Ashley. "Lucky's not here alone. You're meeting someone, right, Lucky? Someone else put the blanket on the fence so you wouldn't get shredded. Isn't that right?" When Lucky didn't answer, Ashley pressed, "So who's here? And don't tell me it's somebody from a gang, 'cause I won't believe you."

Still, no answer.

"Tell me the truth, Lucky," Jack said gently. "I told you before that the truth is really important to me. Is someone waiting for you?"

Softly, so Jack wasn't even sure he heard her, she breathed, "Yes."

"Who?"

"My father." She sighed. "My father's picking me up at Spruce Tree House. And if you think you can make it back to the round house before I get to my dad, you're wrong. I'll be long gone. I'm leaving with him. That's the truth."

She began to move quickly down the winding path. Without saying a word, Jack and Ashley hurried behind until they were walking with her, three abreast. There was nothing the two of them could do but follow her. In its 100-foot descent, the trail switchbacked again and again, and they went down, down, closer to the valley floor.

"Why didn't you just tell the social worker about your dad?" Ashley puffed. "She would have helped you find him."

"Dad doesn't like government organizations."

Thoughts raced through Jack's mind, each one crowding out the other. Lucky had been lying to him all along. Right from the start. The call she made from the pay phone must have been to her father, not to anyone named Maria. It had all been more of her inventions.

"There is no Maria, is there?" he asked. "No gangs, nothing. You were calling your dad, right?"

Lucky jogged around another bend. "I couldn't risk having you know."

"But if there's no gang, what about that bruise? You showed me that mark you said the gang gave you. Where did it come from?"

"It's none of your business." Lucky's voice was suddenly hard.

"Was it your father?" Jack got a sick feeling in his stomach. Maybe that's why Lucky's dad was hiding. Maybe her own father had given her that bruise. As though she could read his thoughts, Lucky said, "That's not it. My dad's never hit me. Ever."

"Then where did it come from?" When she hesitated, Jack grabbed her shoulders. "You're leaving, so what does it matter now if you tell the truth?"

She seemed to want to say something to make them understand, but for once Lucky stumbled for words. "We got separated in Wyoming, and now he's come for me. That's all you need to know."

They'd reached the seep spring, where the people from Spruce Tree House had come to get water nearly a millennium ago. In daylight, the setting of the spring looked like a small amphitheater, a sideways cleft in the surrounding rock, overgrown with leafy scrub. Now, because it lay beyond reach of the moonlight, it appeared as dark as the passage to the underworld, the place the People had risen from on their way to inhabit Earth.

Jack heard a *hiss*. "I think your dad's signaling you," he told Lucky. Turning to face Jack, she answered, "No, not here. We're meeting up at the cliff dwellings."

And then he saw the eyes, the gleaming, golden eyes behind Lucky. And heard again the quiet *hiss*. Moving one silent step at a time, the cougar crept forward toward Lucky's defenseless back.

"Lucky, don't move," Jack commanded, his voice sharp. "For *sure* don't run."

"Why—?"

"Oh my gosh, Jack," Ashley whispered frantically. "It's the one, isn't it? It's coming right at us."

"Ashley, take off the flannel shirt and flap it hard," Jack ordered. When she did, the cougar froze.

Without explaining, Jack fired off his camera, one frame after another in rapid succession, hoping the flash would scare away the big cat. Each burst of light from the flash reflected in the cougar's golden eyes and reflected on something else—something that gleamed on the cougar's neck.

"What are you doing?" Lucky cried, and then she glanced around to see what was behind her.

"Lucky, don't run!" Jack yelled again.

Her face terror stricken, Lucky whirled back toward him and fell onto her knees.

"No!" Jack yelled. "Get up! You've got to get up!"

"I can't!"

The cougar coiled backward as if to spring, snarling and blinking as the flash irritated its eyes.

In panic, Lucky stared at Jack, but she didn't move; it seemed as though she'd frozen into the ground. From the way the big cat's muscles bunched on its shoulders and hindquarters, Jack was sure it would pounce at any moment. Its ribs showed through its fur like the teeth of a comb, and the hollows of its sides were sunken. This cat was hungry. In the animal world, hungry meant fearless. The cougar gave another low *hiss*. Jack took a deep breath and then, inching forward, he gently reached out to raise Lucky to her feet.

"Get behind me!" he whispered.

Now Jack was face to face with the cougar.

Ashley kept flapping the flannel shirt as hard as she could, but that wasn't working, and the camera batteries didn't recover fast enough—too many seconds were elapsing between firings. When the flash did go off one last time, Jack noticed again how it reflected off something on the cougar's neck, but he had no time to think about that. Raising his hands as high as he could and holding his camera upright as if it were a weapon, he slowly waved his arms and stared the big cat straight in the eyes.

Other than its gauntness, it was a magnificent animal, more than a hundred pounds of muscle and sinew beneath a rough, tawny coat. From its nose to the tip of its tail it was six feet long. Ears laid back and eyes narrowed, it snarled at Jack, showing sharp teeth that could bite through a deer's spinal column and kill it instantly. Jack held his ground even though his insides had turned to water.

Just that day he'd picked up a leaflet about cougars at the Balcony House trailhead. Stay calm, it had said, if you come upon a cougar. Move gently. Face the cougar and stand upright. Don't crouch or bend over; do all you can to appear larger. Never block the animal. Make sure it has a route to escape.

The confrontation seemed to last forever. Then, slowly, the cougar began to back up. In a graceful leap, it climbed the rocky overhang above the seep spring and loped away into the night, gliding into the darkness like a vanishing dream.

It was over.

Her voice shaking, Ashley rattled, "I never really liked this flannel shirt of yours before, Jack. I only grabbed it because it was right there and I couldn't reach my jacket, but oh boy, Jack, oh boy"—faster and higher she babbled—"from now on this is my favorite shirt; don't you ever get rid of it, or if you grow out of it, I want it."

"Ashley, take it easy!" Jack told her.

"OK, OK. I just have to say one more thing. Did you see what that cougar had on? A collar."

"What!"

"Yeah, I saw it when the flash went off. A narrow collar with a metal buckle."

So that was what had gleamed on the cougar's neck. A collar!

"Is it gone?" Lucky asked, sobbing and holding her hands over her eyes. "Do I have to keep standing up?" When Jack answered yes, the cougar was gone, and no, she didn't have to stand any longer, she collapsed onto the ground, her forehead on her knees. "This time," she cried, "you *really* saved my life. How can I pay you back?"

Jack was so full of adrenaline from his encounter with a wild beast, so pumped up because he'd known just what to do to scare it off, that he had to come down to earth first before he could even answer Lucky. But he knew what his answer was going to be.

Lucky was trying to leave. If he had any chance of stopping her, he needed one thing. He needed the truth.

CHAPTER NINE

I want the truth about what happened to you." Jack tried to keep his voice calm, even. "About the bruise."

Ashley burst in with, "Jack, we don't have time for this. We've got to tell Mom and Dad about the cougar."

Jack brushed off his sister. The cougar crisis was over for the moment, as far as their safety was concerned. The Lucky crisis would soon move beyond anyone's control unless Jack could stop it. "The truth," he insisted. "Now!"

Lucky took a wavering breath. "You won't understand."

"Try me."

She seemed to weigh something in her mind, hesitating as if she didn't know whether she could trust Jack. Or maybe she was so used to lies, she didn't know how to handle truth.

"If I do tell, I don't want you saying I've got a bad

life or anything like that. Because outsiders just don't get it. The thing is, I'm happy," Lucky went on. "Me and my dad, we go wherever we want. We've been all over the country, all the way up to Canada and down to Florida and California and Texas. So if you want me to talk, don't either one of you say anything about the way we live, all right? Then I'll tell you what you want to know. Is it a deal?" Her voice still shook from the encounter with the cougar, but she seemed willing to talk.

Ashley and Jack nodded. That seemed to satisfy Lucky, because she stopped running her hands up and down her arms as if she were about to peel her sweat-shirt off her skin.

"How about we talk over there," Jack suggested. In the moonlight, where he could see her face. They made their way to an open place where a wall of stone shot into the stars. The three of them leaned against the cool rock, listening as the wind hummed its night song. The breeze lifted the edges of Jack's hair. For a moment all was quiet.

Lucky seemed nervous. "What about the cat?"

"We'll be OK. The cougar's not going to come back. Even if it's still around here, if we stand close together like this, it'll think we're a great big animal, and it'll leave us alone."

"Are you sure?"

"No. But the quicker you talk, the faster we can move out of here."

"OK, OK. Where should I start?" she asked.

"The bruise. This will be the truth, right?"

"Yeah. The truth." She gave Jack a quick glance. Her teeth gleamed when she smiled nervously, but her eyes, shadowed in darkness, were hard to read. "Man, I don't usually have to keep in the lines like this, you know? But OK, I'll try it your way. The first thing you need to understand is that my dad is the best. I mean, he's always thinking of me. When my mom died, my dad tried to keep the two of us going, but he was away all the time working, and I really missed him, and he hated leaving me with strangers. So one day he read about this lady who spilled hot coffee in her lap and sued the restaurant for, like, a million dollars. He started thinking about how much money restaurants pay out for lawsuits, and he got this idea."

It seemed to Jack as though a seawall had been broken, and he was being washed away in a wave of words. Lucky had never spoken with such urgency before. He could tell she really wanted him to sympathize with what she was saying, to comprehend her and her father's life together.

"And so we do this...thing. It's not really bad or anything," Lucky rushed on. "Not when you think about how rich the people are who own stores and restaurants. I mean, have you ever looked at how they live? Have you?"

Jack sensed he was supposed to answer. "No," he said quietly.

"Well, I didn't either till my dad showed me. The owners have huge homes, you know? And they all have insurance, so it doesn't even come out of their pockets or anything. So we—we take a little of their money. Just a tiny little bit. It doesn't hurt them at all."

"You rob stores?" Ashley was incredulous.

"No, that's not what I said."

"Wait a minute, you've lost me, too," Jack told her. "We're talking about bruises. What do they have to do with hot coffee and all of that?"

"I'm getting there. My dad and me—we run a scam."

"A scam?" Ashley asked. "What's a scam?"

"It's a way to get quick money. We go to a store, pretend that I get hurt, and the owner gives my dad money not to sue him."

Even in the half light, Jack saw Ashley's eyebrows crunch together. "Huh?"

"Look, when no one's watching, I spill a little water or soda on the floor, and then I slip on it and fall and make it look so real you'd think I was going to die. Then my dad yells really loud, saying he's going to sue the store 'cause they didn't take care of their property, and his kid got hurt, and he wants a lawyer. And the store owner pays him to take me away. That's our scam."

She shrugged. "I get a few bruises, but it's no big deal. We usually make at least a couple hundred bucks a fall. On the average, more like a thousand. Once we hit it big and got five thousand, but I think that was because the restaurant owner already had some trouble with his license, and he wanted to get rid of us fast." She drew herself up straight so that the moonlight caught her perfect features in outline. "It's like I'm an actress. I've done it for years. And I'm good at it."

To Jack, Lucky sounded not only defiant but proud. It all made sense now. The bruise hadn't come from a gang but from her faking falls while she ripped off store owners. She'd been right; he didn't understand.

Her arms crossed tightly, Ashley asked, "If you and your dad are always together, then why aren't you with him now?"

Lucky answered, "It was stupid. My dad picked out this little hamburger joint, and I did my act perfectly. The guy behind the counter said he was real sorry I got hurt, but the manager was the only one who could give Dad the cash. He said we could come back the next day and collect $500. So my dad argued for a while, then he told the guy we'd be back when they opened up the next morning. But you want to know what that jerk did?"

"What?"

"He called the police. I guess he'd seen me spilling the water, and a camera on the ceiling caught it all. They handcuffed my dad and took him away. As soon as he made bail he got me, and we hit the road. There's a warrant out for him now."

She paused, perhaps debating whether she should

go on. Then she added, "Anyway, we planned on heading for the border. We were on our way, but some cops came into that little truck-stop restaurant in Wyoming. My dad thought they spotted him, so I did my act to get their attention while my dad took off. He's been keeping in touch with me through my pager watch. He pages; I call him. Except—" She frowned. "For a while I didn't hear from him, and I didn't know where he was. He said he'd meet me when we got to the Durango airport, but he didn't show."

"Why not?" Jack asked.

"He told me on the phone tonight. Our car broke down in the middle of nowhere. It's fixed now, though."

Far in the distance a coyote howled at the moon. "That's it. That's my story, and it's the truth," Lucky said, moving away. "You two are the first people I've ever really told it to."

"Well, now I know," Jack said, his voice tight. Her whole explanation had taken only minutes, but Jack felt as though a lifetime's worth of disillusionment had been dumped on him.

Lucky stopped and turned to face him. "You think it's a bad thing we do, don't you? I knew I shouldn't have told you."

"I didn't say anything."

"You didn't have to." Her voice heated up. "You and your sister, living your perfect little lives. You don't know anything about living with your wits and your brains.

My dad and me, we make our own way. If you don't like it, that's your problem."

She moved out of the moonlight and into the shadows again. "Anyway, my dad's waiting."

"One more thing before you go," Ashley said. "What's your real name?"

"Lacey O'Doul," she answered quickly. Then, smiling, she added, "But I like Lucky Deal better, don't you? Well, good-bye. Nice knowing you."

She was a dozen steps away from them when Jack signaled Ashley to follow. They made no secret of it; Lucky had to know they were behind her. She couldn't help hearing their footsteps on the trail. But she kept going, reaching the flat ledge in the alcove where the dwellings stood.

A shadow separated itself from the other shadows as a man stepped forward. "Hi, baby," he said.

"Daddy! I missed you." Lucky wound her arms around the man, and he held her tightly, resting his chin on the top of her head.

It was a tender family reunion. Or was it an act by two con artists? Was there ever anything genuine about Lucky?

"Why are these two kids here?" the man asked.

"I couldn't shake them. They're harmless."

"Will they—?"

"He's OK," Lucky said, pointing to Jack. "He won't talk. The girl—I don't know. But we'll be outta here. Did you bring the flashlight?"

As the man handed her the light, he said, "Use it only where you have to," he said. "When it's dark like this, a light can get spotted from far away."

Lucky crossed the courtyard of the cliff dwellings to peer inside the nearly intact building closest to the trail. "I threw it through there," she said, pointing to a square opening. "I'll have to crawl inside to look for it."

Neither Jack nor Ashley had spoken a word since Lucky met her father. Now Ashley gave Jack a look that meant "I told you all along she'd stolen something from the burn area." Jack nodded grimly.

As Lucky disappeared through the rectangular opening in the ancient wall, the man stood staring at Jack and Ashley. He was dressed all in black—sweater, jeans, running shoes; his pale face seemed disembodied, floating like a mask above the darkness of his husky frame. Never taking his eyes from them, he kept rising on his toes and then rocking back on his heels again and again. To Jack it was a menacing movement, like the coiling of a snake. It made the hair rise on the back of his neck. Ashley stayed very still, breathing shallowly.

"I found it." Lucky's voice sounded muffled from inside the stone walls. "I knew I would." As she crawled back through the opening with the flashlight in her right hand, her left hand tightly clutched something small enough to fit in her fist.

"Take a look," she said, shining the flashlight on her open palm. "It ought to be worth plenty, Dad."

Jack moved forward to get a look, too. Lucky was holding a piece of turquoise, a little more than an inch square. With a few skillful lines in the polished surface, the ancient carver had created the unmistakable figure of a frog.

"A fetish," Jack said, speaking for the first time. "For one of the gods."

"Really old, right?" Lucky exulted.

"Uh-huh."

"Old things like this are super valuable. We made another hit, Dad. This time it's our biggest yet!"

"It is ancient," Jack agreed. "And if you had papers or anything to show you got it from Mesa Verde, it might be worth something." He took a breath. "But the problem is, you can't prove it came from here. You can't prove anything about it. So for you, it's worthless."

"What do you mean?" Both Lucky and her father turned on him with such vehemence that Jack took a step back.

"Look at it," he stammered. "It could have been carved yesterday. Turn it over—I bet there's no mark to show how old it is, right? I've seen lots of fetishes just like this in gift shops. There's one for sale in Jackson Hole. About a hundred dollars."

"Turn off the flashlight," Lucky's father commanded, scowling at Jack. "Is that true?"

Jack's voice wavered. "Ask Lucky if I tell the truth."

Grudgingly, Lucky answered, "Always." And Ashley added, "For sure."

"So why don't you just leave it here?" Jack pleaded with Lucky. "Like I said, you couldn't sell it for much because there's no way to date it, but the park archaeologists can use it to study the Puebloan culture. To them it's really important. A piece of the puzzle." When Lucky didn't answer, he pressed, "Besides, a fetish is, like, holy to the Native American people. Come on, Lucky, leave it with me. I'll make sure it gets to the park staff. It's the right thing to do."

Lucky wavered, but her father told her, "Keep it, baby. We'll show it to a pawn dealer and check it out. You might trust this kid, but I don't. Anyway, let's get out of here. This place gives me the shakes. Too many ghosts spooking around."

It took only a minute for Lucky to answer. "I'm keeping it," she told Jack coolly. "My dad's right. I found it, and that makes it mine." And then, to her father, "Let's go."

Brushing past Jack, Lucky grabbed the man's hand as the two of them descended the path, chattering about the cougar and her near escape. Her father told her not to worry. No big cat would dare mess with him, he said, and if one did, he had a long switchblade in his pocket.

Jack and Ashley stood silently as they watched Lucky's white sweatshirt shrink to the size of a postage stamp. What should he do? Jack wondered. Follow them, maybe try to stop Lucky on his own? No, Lucky's dad said he had a knife. Jack couldn't risk tangling with him and possibly getting himself or Ashley hurt. Besides, the man was at least 70 pounds heavier and half a foot taller than Jack. No way could Jack overpower him. There was not a thing he could do but watch them disappear. Suddenly, Lucky's pleasant voice called back to Jack, like a leaf floating on a breeze.

"Hey Jack, you better grab your sister and catch up with us. You guys need that blanket to climb the fence, and my dad's taking it with him."

"I don't know if we should," Ashley murmured. "Her dad's a crook."

Jack said, "We've got to go. We don't want to be stuck here with a cougar."

"Last chance!" Lucky called again.

Jack cupped his hands around his mouth. "Wait up. We're coming."

As they hurried after the two people in the lead, Jack rattled assurances to Ashley that they'd be OK, that most of all they needed to get back to the round house. There was no way over the barbed wire without the blanket. He was a little surprised that Lucky even cared enough to keep the blanket in place for them.

Once they caught up to her, she didn't look at them, but instead kept her eyes on her father as he hoisted her up and over, followed by Ashley, then Jack. Finally, Lucky's father scaled the fence easily and hopped down onto the asphalt path. He pulled the blanket off the barbed wire, ripping tufts of cotton from it in the spots where the wire had held it fast.

"Don't want to leave this thing," he told Lucky. "I keep it in the trunk. Comes in handy, like when the car broke down, and I had to crawl under it." He slung the blanket over his shoulder like a serape.

"Let's take off now," he said. "I parked just off Mesa Top Loop Road, so we'll need to hike around the rim above Spruce Tree House to get to the car. There's a trail. How does your smart dad know all this? I got some topo maps in Cortez and plotted everything out. What do I always tell you, baby?"

"Use your head and plan ahead."

"That's right. Glad you didn't forget it while you were hanging out with the Boy Scout here. We'll be following that second trail until we can cut into those back woods." Pointing across the valley to the moon-lit cliffs, Lucky's dad spoke as if neither Landon was even there. "See, baby? Back behind that ledge. We're almost home free."

"What about them?" Lucky asked. Jack knew exactly who "them" referred to. Ashley stiffened beside him.

"Oh, we'll be long gone before they can alert any-one. Besides," he said, focusing on Ashley and Jack, "you two wouldn't want to keep our little family apart, now, would you?"

Ashley's voice was barely above a whisper. "No."

"Good. That's just what I thought."

They continued silently up the last part of the trail until it intersected with the main path. Above them, park buildings loomed like big square blocks, checkering the grounds with shadows.

"OK. This is where I came in," Lucky told her dad. "Jack and Ashley followed from up there."

"You kids know how to get back where you're going?" he asked.

"Yes," Jack answered.

"Good. Well then, I guess this makes it good-bye. Adios, amigos. Thanks for taking care of my girl." With that, he grabbed Lucky's hand and pulled her up to a narrower portion of the trail, which wound through a patch of gnarled trees. In only a moment they were out of sight.

CHAPTER TEN

Jack stood frozen. So that was it. He'd never see Lucky again. His mind choked on thoughts of Lucky's future and how she was about to be sucked back into a life where people were nothing more than marks and stealing was normal. It was like watching someone drown in cold, churning water while he just stood there, afraid to do anything about it. He made himself sick.

"Come on, Jack. We've got to tell Mom and Dad," Ashley pleaded.

"You tell them. Tell them about the cougar and about Lucky. I'm going after her." It was as though someone else were inside his head, moving his mouth and speaking for him, and yet, unnatural as it felt, he knew the internal voice was right. He had to try.

"Are you *crazy?*"

"Yeah. Probably. Absolutely." He grabbed her elbow and shoved her in the direction of the round house.

"Go get help, Jack pleaded."

Ashley's eyes narrowed with anger and fear. "Forget it! I'm not going without you."

"Yes you are."

"You can't make me!"

"Ashley—"

"I'll follow you."

"Hold on," Jack began, trying to soothe her. "Listen to me. The longer I stand here arguing with you the farther away they get. I'm the only one who can maybe talk her into staying. You know that's the truth. You know what kind of life she'll go back to. Let me at least try. Ashley, I need to try."

"But he said he had a knife."

Jack tried to push down the cold feeling that welled up inside him. Better not to think about that. Time was ticking quickly, and he had to move. "Mom and Dad might have checked on us, in which case they're probably freaking out by now. You've got to let them know what's happened. So go." When Ashley didn't budge, he yelled, "Go!" loud enough that she scampered away, calling over her shoulder as she ran, "I'll do it, but I'm bringing them back with me. You be careful, Jack!"

The trail that Lucky and her dad had taken petered into a thin, washed-out dirt path. Spruce Tree House was nestled on a ledge in the east side of a giant bowl. Lucky and her father now circled around the north part of the bowl, heading east, toward the overhang above the dwellings.

By tracking Lucky's white sweatshirt, Jack could spot them in the moonlight, and they were already far ahead. If he was going to catch her, he'd have to move fast.

Even though the drop to his right was sheer enough to kill, Jack began to run the trail, stumbling over small rocks that blended into the powdery soil, at times lurching wildly as he maneuvered his way along the rim. He could hear them up ahead; the wind had stopped, and in the stillness their voices carried as clearly as if they'd all been in a room together.

Lucky was laughing about the shape of the rock formation the trail cut through. The path ran through solid rock, a thin wedge that looked as though a slice had been removed from a long loaf of bread.

"Go sideways, Dad," she said.

"I am," he said. "Blast, this thing is narrow. What is this anyway?"

"The tour guide said the park carved it into the rock so rainwater would run through it and not drip down on the cliff dwellings. To keep them from eroding, you know? This park is a really cool place, Dad."

"Well, this slice in the rock makes a heck of a tight fit for me. Just a little farther, baby, and then it's into the woods and on to our next adventure. Wait a second." His voice sharpened with a new urgency. "Behind us. Someone's coming."

It was impossible for Jack to go both quickly and quietly, so he fumbled his way to the runoff canal and bolted through it. In the middle the channel was nearly as deep as he was tall and so black with shadow that he couldn't see his feet.

"Who's there?" The voice of Lucky's father rang with menace. "I'm asking just one more time. Who is it?"

Jack took a deep breath. "It's me. Jack. I want to talk to Lucky. I'm alone," he said as he emerged from the channel.

"What do you think you're doing? Get out of here!" Lucky cried.

"Just hear me out. Please."

"No. We've already talked. Leave me alone." Moving up and over a layer of sandstone that looked as smooth as ice cream, Lucky hurried away from Jack.

"Give me one minute to tell you something really important!"

"Get away! I'm not giving it back. It's mine, and I'm going to sell it."

"You heard what the girl said," her father threatened, and then, "Lucky, come over here, you're getting off the trail."

"No, no. Wait," Jack protested. "I don't want to talk about the fetish." It was as though he and Lucky were opposite magnets—every move he made to get close to her propelled her in another direction.

"Baby, don't go that way," her father warned as he

slipped on some loose rock. He wasn't as quick as his daughter, which meant Jack had just a fraction of time to say why he'd come. An instant of time to make his case.

"Lucky, remember when you said that you'd never really known people who were honest before? Remember? I think you'd like to be one of those people. I think deep down you want a regular life. Isn't that true?"

He could see her now; she'd turned to face him down. Ahead of her beckoned a forest of pinyon pine and juniper that would hide Lucky and her father in an instant. Behind her loomed the canyon. She stood, head high, on the rim of rock, as though she were the masthead of a ship.

"What do you want?"

"I want you to think about coming back with me. Stay with us. You can go to school and eat pizza on Friday nights and go to the mall and watch stupid movies and just...just live. Come back with me, and you can be like every other kid."

"You mean be like you."

"Yes. No! I mean you can have fun, and just be."

Lucky's voice was steady in the darkness. "I have my own life. I told you, I make my own way."

Her father had stopped moving, maybe wanting to hear what his daughter would say. Although Jack felt the man's presence, he kept his own eyes locked on Lucky.

"Lucky, what you're doing is wrong."

"Wrong?" she spat. "Who are you, Jack, to tell me

that? There's no such thing as wrong. You've got your rule book, and I've got mine. I'm willing to play my own game. My game, my choice."

"But—"

In that instant, a bright light shot on, illuminating, like the tail of a comet, the ground all the way across the canyon. A man's voice boomed above the chasm: *"Hold it right there! All of you!"*

Jack thought he could make out a ranger hat and park uniform, although the man stood too far away to be sure.

"Dad!" Lucky cried. "It's the cops! Run!" Spinning, she tried to bolt for the trees, but loose gravel sputtered out from underneath her sandals and she fell, rolling toward the ledge behind her.

"Dad! Help me! Jack! Please! Help me!"

"Don't move! Baby...don't—"

A scream pierced the air, freezing the marrow in Jack's bones. "No!" he shouted, running toward her. He was too late.

Lucky had gone over the edge.

CHAPTER ELEVEN

Lucky!" Jack screamed.

His legs pumping with adrenaline, Jack raced to the spot on the ledge where he thought he'd seen Lucky fall. The edge dropped beneath his feet; for an instant he felt he might go over himself before he skidded to a stop. He teetered back and forth, then dropped to his knees. Fear swept into his throat and clamped it so tight he could hardly breathe as he peered into the blackness below, afraid of what he knew he would see. She could never survive from that height. All that would be left would be a broken body.

"Help me! Help me!"

He'd been mistaken—she'd fallen farther to the left! Relief let his lungs start taking in air again. Two feet below the rim a patch of jagged stone stuck into the air like gnarled fingers. Lucky had clamped onto the rock so tightly her knuckles gleamed in the moonlight.

He couldn't see her face, just the top of her head pinched between her arms, and her hair flaming out in twists of auburn.

"Hold on!" Jack commanded, flopping onto his stomach. Leaning over as far as he dared, he grasped her wrist and pulled with everything he had. It was a mistake. His abrupt motion caused her remaining hand to lose its grip, and suddenly she was dangling from one arm with Jack the only force keeping her from certain death.

Too terrified to say anything, Lucky gave out a piercing scream.

He couldn't believe how heavy she was. His own body slid a sliver at a time toward the edge. Rocks bit into his stomach, and he felt his shoulders being pulled from their sockets. The muscles in his back strained to hold her, working against weight that felt like lead. His biceps shook with effort as he pulled, but his hands were sweating and the skin of her wrist slipped beneath his fingers, a quarter inch at a time. He knew he couldn't hold on.

"Daddy!" Lucky screamed. *"Help me, Daddy. Help me!"*

"I'm here, baby. Don't look down. Don't look!"

Lucky's father thrust his arms down along the rock face. Grabbing beneath where Jack's hands gripped Lucky's wrist, in one swift movement he had her halfway up over the rock ledge. Then he grasped the waistband of her shorts and lifted her the rest of the way to safety.

Lucky was scraped from her shins to her thighs and crying hysterically. She collapsed into her father's arms; if he hadn't held her upright, she'd have fallen.

"I thought for sure I was going to die!" she sobbed. "In the dark!"

"It's OK. You're OK now. Let's get away from the edge. You're all right," her father crooned, wrapping the blanket around her shoulders.

Jack's mouth tasted like metal, and he realized he was breathing hard, in and out, as though he'd just run a mile. As far as Lucky and her father were concerned, he'd become invisible. Lucky's father had his chin on top of her head and was holding her tight, rocking her from side to side, cocooned in the blanket. Jack didn't blame her dad for forgetting in the near tragedy that Jack, too, had been part of the rescue.

Suddenly, Lucky reached out to grab Jack, pulling him close. She clung to his neck.

He felt a slap on his back, not hostile, but grateful— man to man. "You saved my daughter. I...I can't even begin to...to....I wouldn't have made it to her in time, you know," her father told him. "I don't say this often. Maybe not nearly enough. But thank you. Thank you for my girl."

Maybe they'd forgotten about the park ranger. That worry likely got shoved way to the bottom of their priority list when Lucky fell. Suddenly, a light hit the three of them like a beacon.

"Stand still. I have a few questions, starting with you, sir. I'd like to see some identification."

The law enforcement ranger was a Navajo. Tall and burly, he had a round, bronzed face framed by gray hair mostly hidden beneath his ranger's hat. The man commanded authority, and not just because of his height or his uniform.

Lucky's dad flashed him a huge grin. "I'm sure glad to see you, officer. We've had a bit of a scare. My girl here almost fell off the ledge."

"Just being here is extremely dangerous," the ranger said severely. "You're not allowed in this area. The park sites are closed for the night, and this one's off limits even in the daytime."

"Of course, officer, I know that. But my daughter Amanda's a wild thing." Then, conspiratorially, he added, "You know how teenagers are—turn your back for one minute and they're getting into all kinds of mischief. You got any kids?"

"Daddy," Lucky whined, "I already said I was sorry for sneaking out. It's my fault, officer," she told the ranger. "My dad followed me here. I'll never do it again, I promise."

Amanda? A fake name, same as Deal. Smooth and in control, Lucky played this situation like a pro. No one would ever guess that just a moment earlier she'd been sobbing hysterically.

But the ranger was more interested in the man

standing in front of him. He pointed to the flashlight hanging from Lucky's father's belt. "I got a call about someone breaking into Spruce Tree House. Someone with a light. Would that be you?"

"Me?" His voice sounded innocent enough. "No, not me. I was just up here getting my daughter back. She was meeting her boyfriend." Shrugging his shoulders, he said, "Kids. What are you going to do?"

The ranger's light practically blinded Jack as it hit him full in the face. They were using him in their alibi, and that was wrong. Yet the words to expose them stayed in his mouth. Up until he'd met Lucky, Jack had known right from wrong—moral questions had always been an easy call for him. Suddenly, doing the right thing had a price attached: To tell what he knew would mean Lucky's father would go to jail, and she would be alone. But wasn't that exactly what Jack had wanted? Yes, he told himself. And at the same time, no. It was supposed to be Lucky's choice, not something forced on her. It was too much to sift through. He stayed silent.

The light swiveled back to Lucky's father. "Sir, you still haven't shown me your ID."

"Of course. I apologize. I guess I just got to chatting." Lucky's father made a show of patting down his back pocket. "Where's my wallet? Oh, I can't believe it," he groaned. "It must have slipped out of my pocket and gone over the cliff while I was pulling up my daughter." Sighing deeply, he glared at Lucky. "Amanda, look at the trouble your little escapade's caused. First, you almost get yourself killed, and now my wallet's gone."

"Sorry, Daddy." Lucky's voice was contrite.

"Officer, as you can see, I don't have my ID, although it's through no fault of my own. Could I ask a favor of you? Is it possible you could help me look down on the valley floor for my billfold? I hate to leave it here the rest of the night," he said with an easy laugh. "Some wild animal might carry it off. I heard there's cougars around here. You know, with that big light of yours we have a chance to find my wallet. I'd really appreciate your help." Once again, that easy grin.

Jack knew he would have been fooled by the charade, but the ranger kept his face stony. "With no ID, I have no choice but to take the three of you to headquarters," he announced. "The administration building reported that they saw someone in Spruce Tree House, someone with a flashlight. You're here, and you've got a flashlight."

"But officer," Lucky pleaded, "that wasn't us. Honest!"

Lucky's father narrowed his eyes. His voice had suddenly cooled. "You can't take us in. That's an abuse of power. You have no legal grounds—"

"There's trespassing, for starters. I can hold you on that until we determine who you are and ascertain if there are any damages at Spruce Tree," the ranger replied. "We're all going to leave together until I can sort this out. And in case you get any ideas, you might want to know that I've already called for backup. They'll join us any minute now."

Jack saw the look that passed between Lucky and her dad. It seemed they could communicate without words, with just slight nods and gestures. "All right, come on, Amanda," he said. "Take my hand so you won't slip."

As they moved toward the trail, Lucky's feet suddenly shot out from underneath her, and she landed hard on the rocky ledge.

"Oh, I'm hurt, I'm hurt!" she screamed.

"Amanda! What's wrong?" Lucky's father bent over her.

"It's my ankle—I think it's broken!"

Jack didn't know what to believe. He ran to her side, crouching over her writhing body. "Lucky, are you OK?"

Without answering, she clutched his hand in hers. Her wide eyes fixed on his as she pressed something into his palm, something small and cold and smooth. For a split second she stopped crying, and it seemed to Jack as if he were in the eye of a hurricane. Then, almost as quickly as she'd stopped, Lucky started howling again.

When the ranger gently pressed her ankle, Lucky shrieked in pain.

"I don't think it's broken," the ranger told them, gingerly pulling his hand away. "It might be a sprain, though. I'd better radio for medical help."

Lucky's father pulled her to her feet, telling her to

try to put a little weight on it just to see if she could stand, all the while yelling at the ranger that he'd better get some assistance up here right away since this was all his fault, and Amanda ought to sue the entire Mesa Verde law enforcement department because they were responsible for this accident, no doubt about it.

The ranger pulled out his two-way radio and began to talk to someone. It must have been the moment Lucky and her dad had been waiting for, because in that split second the two of them sprinted into the tangle of pinyon and juniper forest. Lucky ran as quickly and gracefully as an antelope; there was nothing wrong with her ankle, just as Jack had suspected. The blanket over her shoulders made it impossible to see her once she hit the cover of the trees.

"Hey!" the ranger cried, whirling around. "Stop! Get back here!"

He had a gun strapped to his belt, and for one horrifying second Jack imagined the man might pull it out and shoot, but the gun never left its holster. Instead, the ranger started to race into the woods after Lucky and her father, yelling for them to stop while his flashlight swept the trees like the beam of a lighthouse.

Not knowing what to do, Jack waited. Moments later the ranger came back, shaking his head. "They're gone," he told him. "With all this forest for camouflage, I can't find them. Do you know which way they're headed?"

"I don't know," Jack told him. "But we were in

Spruce Tree House. And we saw a cougar down by the spring. I think it's the killer."

"What?" the ranger sounded incredulous.

"It had a collar on, and it looked hungry," Jack said woodenly. "That ought to identify it. You should be able to catch it now."

"Wait a minute—are you lying?"

"No."

"Because that's a serious thing to say. The whole park's been in an uproar over this cougar problem, and your friends just ran off like a couple of criminals, which I'm guessing they are. How do you fit into all this? Are you really the boyfriend?"

Jack opened his hand and saw the turquoise fetish Lucky had put there. In the moonlight it gleamed a delicate blue-green.

"Yes," he answered softly. "I guess I am."

CHAPTER TWELVE

W hat did the collar look like?" Olivia was asking. "Was it a tracking collar like they use on the wolves at Yellowstone?"

"No—a dog collar," Ashley answered. "The kind you can buy at Kmart. Not real wide, but it had a big buckle."

The four Landons were back at the round house. Olivia spoke into a two-way radio the Navajo ranger had given her, relaying Ashley's information to the searchers in the field. It was now three in the morning, and the whole park staff was out in force, trying to locate the dangerous cat.

No one was bothering to look for Lucky or her father, not even the local police. Since manpower was at a premium and the two O'Douls were not considered to be a threat, the search for them had been shoved to the back burner. Until tomorrow, maybe, or at least till the cougar had been caught.

Olivia snapped off the radio and let out a big sigh. "Finally, it makes sense," she said. "You've solved it, Ashley—that collar means the cougar wasn't wild. Someone had raised it as a pet—found it when it was a cute little cub and kept it penned up. Then it grew big and got too hard to handle, so the owner let it loose. Probably brought it here to the park and set it free."

Jack nodded. "So that's why it wasn't afraid of people. It came straight up to us."

"Right. It was used to the smell of humans and connected that scent with being fed. When the owner dumped it, the poor animal had trouble fending for itself in the wild."

"Yeah, it looked kind of skinny," Ashley broke in.

"Because it had never been taught by its mother to hunt," Olivia continued. "It probably didn't even know how to find water."

A signal from the two-way radio made them all turn to stare at it. Switching it on, Olivia said, "Yes?"

"We've got it," the radio-transmitted voice announced. "The cat with the collar. Thought you'd want to know, Dr. Landon."

"Good. What are you going to—" The unmistakable crack of rifle fire exploded through the receiver in Olivia's hand. Jack flinched, Steven bit his lip, and Ashley's eyes filled with tears. "It's all over, Dr. Landon," the voice said. "We found our cougar, thanks to those kids of yours."

Ashley sobbed, "Oh Mom, I didn't want to—"

Olivia reached to comfort her daughter. "I hate it too, honey," she said. "But we had no choice. Once animals have been raised by humans, they rarely adapt to life in the wild. And when they start attacking people, like that little boy and that woman—"

"But those people are going to be OK, right?"

"Yes, they're both going to be fine. But the next person might not have been so lucky. This simply had to be done, Ashley."

"At least the rest of the cougars in the park will be left in peace," Steven told her.

Ashley cried, "Still, I have this big ache inside."

Jack did too. A huge ache. And only part of it was because of the cougar. That part would heal over time, but the rest of the hurt would be with him always.

Even in June in Jackson Hole, the peaks of the Tetons glistened with snow. In the valley it was shorts and T-shirt weather.

School was out, and Steven had come home for lunch, bringing tacos. The three of them—Olivia was at work at the elk refuge—sat at their picnic table in the backyard munching the crispy taco shells. Jack liked hot sauce on his beef-and-bean hardshell taco; Ashley preferred sour cream and guacamole on hers.

As he ate, Jack read the sports pages. The Utah Jazz were playing in the finals for the NBA championship.

Ordinarily this would have fired him with excitement, but now he put down the paper with only half the columns read.

"I see the mail truck out front," Ashley said. "I'll go get the mail."

"No, I will." For two weeks Jack had tried to be first at the mailbox every day, hoping in vain for even a postcard from Lucky. Now he came back and handed half a dozen bills and advertisements to his father.

Steven opened one envelope and frowned. "I don't get this," he said. "This phone bill has calls on it that we didn't make."

Jack sat up straighter. "Like what?"

"Starting with—one from here at the house at 2 a.m. on the night before we left for Mesa Verde. That has to be a mistake."

"Where's it to?" Jack asked, remembering that middle-of-the-night phone call when he first heard about the fictitious Maria.

"To Moab, Utah. We don't even know anyone in Moab. And here's one made from Mesa Verde to Cortez, Colorado—it's billed to your mother's phone card."

That's where Lucky's father had been that evening— Cortez, just down the road from the park. "Lucky calling her dad," Ashley murmured.

Steven may not have heard her, because he went on, "And the day after that, there was a call from Santa Fe, New Mexico, and then another one from Albuquerque.

Both of these calls were charged to the phone card."

"Heading south," Jack said.

Steven hadn't been ignoring the obvious. "They were on their way to the Mexican border," he said. "There's a call from El Paso, Texas, and this last one is an international call, from Ciudad Juárez." He threw down the bundle of mail. "So they made it to Mexico. I don't know whether I'm glad or sorry. That poor kid, Lucky—what kind of life is she going to have, always on the run, in a different country with no family, no friends—"

She has one friend, Jack thought. No matter where she is.

"Who were the calls made to?" Ashley asked.

"I don't know. I'd have to get in touch with the phone company, I guess, to find out. Maybe I ought to give the information to Ms. Lopez," Steven decided. "Not that it will do any good now that Lucky and her father are in Mexico. But I suppose I do need to report it. Poor Ms. Lopez had quite a time with Lucky—trying to track her name and checking out that white tiger story, which, of course, turned out to be just another one of Lucky's tales. Who knows, maybe Lucky will turn out to be a writer." Untangling his long legs from the picnic bench, Steven stood up and went into the house.

Jack had saved one letter from the day's mail because it was addressed to him. The return address said Mesa Verde National Park. Picking up a dinner knife, he sliced open the flap on the envelope.

"Dear Jack Landon," the letter began, "We wish to express our deep appreciation to you for returning the turquoise frog fetish to the museum association. When you gave it to us, you expressed the opinion that the fetish, although old, didn't have an especially great financial value. It is correct that small stone carvings cannot usually be dated because they are noncarbon-based materials—"

"What does that mean?" Ashley asked, pointing to the line Jack was reading.

He jerked the paper away. "Who said you could read my mail?"

"Oh, come on, Jack. I was as much a part of that night as you were. What to they mean about the dating?"

He sighed. "Carbon dating only works on things that were once living—like the fiber in sandals, or the turkey-feather blankets the People made, or old bones. Not on stone or turquoise or anything that wasn't alive. Now back off while I finish reading this."

He turned his attention to the letter in his hand.

"...noncarbon-based materials," he continued. "How-ever, it happens that this turquoise fetish is different. As we examined it, we realized it had once held tiny gemstones for eyes. The gemstones are long gone, but residue remains of the pitch that was used to glue the eyes in place. And pitch, because it comes from pine trees, can be dated. Very preliminary test results lead us to believe that this fetish was made approximately 780 years ago. Since its age can be certified, the piece is priceless. Of course, even if it had little financial value, the fetish would be invaluable to us as an artifact that expands our knowledge of the prehistoric Puebloan culture. For that reason, we extend to you our heartfelt thanks. Sincerely, Linda Martin, Curator."

In a handwritten note at the bottom of the letter, she'd added, "Just for fun, Jack, if I had to put a price on the fetish, I'd guess about a quarter million dollars."

Jack closed his eyes and leaned back so far he nearly fell off the bench.

"Can I see it now?" Ashley asked. He handed it to her.

"Wow!" Ashley jumped up, waving the letter. "Wow! Lucky would curl up and die if she knew about this— a quarter million! Wow!"

"She would have given it back anyway, because it belonged in the park," Jack insisted.

Ashley laughed so hard Jack felt a slow burn crawling up his cheeks. "Oh yeah! Sure she would, Jack! You are some dreamer. She thought it was worth about a hundred bucks, so she gave it back. But a quarter million? No way!"

Steven came out of the house then. "They can't trace Lucky and her dad from the phone calls they made," he said. "The calls were just to sporting-goods stores and travel offices and places like that. I guess they drove from El Paso across the border into Juárez. Ms. Lopez says she'll call the border checkpoints, but she suspects

O'Doul was an alias, too. They probably used lots of different names, and had several different passports."

"Dad, you might want to see this," Jack said. He handed his father the letter from Mesa Verde. Without another word, Jack went inside.

CHAPTER THIRTEEN

He'd been waiting for a chance to be alone in the house. That evening, at last, his mother and dad and Ashley had gone to a movie. Jack had begged off, saying he was halfway through a book more exciting than any movie playing in Jackson Hole that week.

Eighteen days had passed since Lucky had run away from him, disappearing into the forest on top of the mesa. In all that time, his film had remained inside his camera, untouched.

He hadn't been trying for pictures when he fired his camera's flash at the cougar. All he'd wanted was to scare the big cat, to make it go away. He hadn't pointed the camera, he hadn't focused, he'd just pressed the shutter button to make the automatic flash go off. Later, when he looked at the number showing how far the film had advanced, he discovered he'd clicked the shutter 14 times. No wonder the flash had stopped recharging.

Fourteen wild, random shots. What were the odds that he'd captured something on film? Anything? As he made his way to the basement to his father's darkroom, he held his hopes in check.

After filling the tanks with water and chemicals, he turned off the lights and loaded the film onto the processing spool. As he worked, he kept checking the glow-in-the-dark numbers on the clock they used to time steps in the developing process. He wanted everything finished before his parents and Ashley came home.

As he took the roll of negatives from the stabilizer solution, he caught his breath. He didn't want to look too closely—not yet—but he may have lucked out on at least two frames. Don't get your hopes up, he told himself.

Negatives dried. Paper in the developing tube. Jack checked the clock again, sending mental signals to his parents to take Ashley for ice cream after the movie. When at last he allowed himself to really look at his prints, his heart thudded.

Twelve of them were useless. They showed slabs of rock, bits of trees, the cougar's left front foot, half of its face—or nothing at all.

But one! One was a magnificent shot of the cougar in full snarl. Each whisker stood out against the dark background. The pink nose and the ridge of fur behind it wrinkled menacingly. And the eyes—the flash had caught them full on, so that they gleamed like beacons.

It was an almost perfect picture. Later, Jack would show it to his father, who would probably blow it up to poster size in the studio where he worked.

Then, as if he might be handling the Grail, Jack turned his attention to the picture that mattered most, the one he'd been hoping against all odds would turn out to be good.

Gently, holding the wet print only by the edges, he gazed into Lucky's face. She stared back at him, startled by the camera's flash. It was just before she'd turned to discover the cougar; she didn't yet wear the expression of terror that would twist her features just a few seconds afterward.

For a long time he stared at her, remembering the good things about her—her smile, the time in the tunnel when she'd taken his hand, the way she'd secretly passed the piece of turquoise to him just before she fled. It hurt to think that the good in her might never have a chance to grow.

All he had of her was this picture. And no one else was ever going to see it.

AFTERWORD

In my job as a park ranger at Mesa Verde National Park, I get to drive up onto this amazing mesa every day. One spring morning, just after 7 a.m., I had a terrific wildlife sighting—a cougar! He stood just above the road on a small slope. I looked at him, and he looked at me. Cougars, also called mountain lions, are mostly nocturnal hunters, so perhaps this lion was returning from a hunting trip in search of his favorite food: mule deer.

He stood on the slope in the morning sunshine, tawny brown, probably six feet long, his graceful tail a full one-third of his body length. Beautiful and awe inspiring, he probably weighed around 170 pounds of sleek, fluid strength. As I watched, his ears perked up, and he seemed to look me right in the eyes. It sent a chill running up my spine. Almost before I realized what I had seen, he was gone.

Except for the paved road, my sighting could have

been exactly like the sighting of an Ancestral Puebloan some 700 years ago. The same sun was shining on that person along a dirt trail near the edge of the same canyon. An ancestor of the cougar I saw could have stood in the same place and inspired the same feelings. Across the centuries I felt a kinship with those residents of Mesa Verde, human and mountain lion alike.

Unfortunately, since A.D. 1300 (when most people had left Mesa Verde), not everyone has felt that same kinship with the cougar. As European settlers, farmers, and ranchers moved across North America, the cougar has been pushed from its homeland, which ranged from coast to coast, from Canada to Mexico. Fear for their livestock and even for their own families has caused people to kill cougars and other predators, wherever people came into contact with wildlife. Encroaching development across the West—cities, towns, houses, ranches—destroyed habitat for the cougar. People need places to live and work, but cougars have the same needs. Cougars now live mostly in the West, pushed into islands of wilderness like Mesa Verde National Park.

Our natural fear of the cougar is not without cause. Cougars attacking people, as in this book, are events that are rare, but they do happen. You are much more likely to be attacked by another person than by a cougar. Yet when cougar attacks do occur, it's big news in newspapers and magazines, and on the radio and TV.

Mesa Verde kids probably also heard stories about

cougars when they lived in places like Cliff Palace, Balcony House, and Spruce Tree House. During the winter, around the warming fire of their clan's kiva, these kids probably listened to cougar stories from their grand-parents. The People didn't have a written history, so stories, religion, and a strong understanding of their own family history were all passed on from one generation to the next by word of mouth. As they went to sleep at night, the children were probably afraid of the cougar, but they also would have felt that it was a natural part of their world, an animal to be respected and revered.

Mesa Verde National Park is an important place for all of us, cougars and people alike, to share our common history going back thousands of years. We need public lands to ensure habitat for all wildlife and to ensure that all of the dwellings and artifacts of earlier people are preserved for future generations.

When you have the opportunity to visit a national park, please remember that everything you find there is protected—plants, animals, rocks, artifacts, everything. You're welcome to take photographs, like Jack, and to take away as much litter as you can carry.

Come explore Mesa Verde National Park. Look back in time to the places where kids lived 700 years ago. Who knows? You just might see a cougar!

Will Morris
Chief of Interpretation and Visitor Services
Mesa Verde National Park, Mesa Verde, Colorado

DON'T MISS—

WOLF STALKER
MYSTERY #1

Fast-paced adventure has the Landons on the trail
of an injured wolf in Yellowstone National Park.

COMING SOON—

DEADLY WATERS
MYSTERY #3

RAGE OF FIRE
MYSTERY #4

THE HUNTED
MYSTERY #5

GHOST HORSES
MYSTERY #6

ABOUT THE AUTHORS

An award-winning mystery writer and an award-winning science writer—who are also mother and daughter—are working together on Mysteries in Our National Parks!

Alane (Lanie) Ferguson's first mystery, *Show Me the Evidence,* won the Edgar Award, given by the Mystery Writers of America.

Gloria Skurzynski's *Almost the Real Thing* won the American Institute of Physics Science Writing Award.

Lanie lives in Elizabeth, Colorado. Gloria lives in Salt Lake City, Utah. To work together on a novel, they connect by phone, fax, and e-mail and "often forget which one of us wrote a particular line."

Gloria's e-mail: gloriabooks@qwest.net

Her Web site: http://gloriabooks.com

Lanie's e-mail: aferguson@sprynet.com

The world's largest nonprofit scientific and educational organization, the National Geographic Society was founded in 1888 "for the increase and diffusion of geographic knowledge." Since then it has supported scientific exploration and spread information to its more than eight million members worldwide. The National Geographic Society educates and inspires millions every day through magazines, books, television programs, videos, maps and atlases, research grants, the National Geographic Bee, teacher workshops, and innovative classroom materials. The Society is supported through membership dues, charitable donations, and income from the sale of its educational products. Members receive NATIONAL GEOGRAPHIC magazine—the Society's official journal—discounts on Society products and other benefits. For more information about the National Geographic Society, its educational programs and publications, and ways to support its work, please call 1-800-NGS-LINE (647-5463), or write to the following address:

NATIONAL GEOGRAPHIC SOCIETY

1145 17th Street N.W.

Washington, D.C. 20036-4688

U.S.A.

Visit the Society's Web site: www.nationalgeographic.com